'You can't stay here. I won't let you.'

'Oh, really?' She raised her brows. 'I don't see that you have a choice. It's my decision to make, not yours.'

'Is it? Maybe I can persuade you otherwise…'

Before Rebecca had time to realise Cade's intention he swooped, claiming her mouth in a fierce, possessive kiss that caused the blood to course through her body in an overwhelming tide of heat. Her lips parted beneath the sensual onslaught and she clung to him as her limbs responded by trembling under the passionate intensity of his embrace.

It was like nothing she'd ever experienced before. His kisses made her feverish with desire, the touch of his hands turned her flesh to fire as they shaped her curves, leaving her desperate for more. It was so unexpected, such a coaxing, tantalising raid on her defences. Her resistance crumbled. She wanted to stay here, locked in his arms, having him hold her, his long, hard body pressuring hers and promising her heaven on earth.

Dear Reader,

What better place is there to while away the hours than on a beautiful Caribbean island? The gentle lap of surf on the sand, palm trees swaying in a soft, warm breeze…In this idyllic setting a girl can surely soak up the sun and forget her troubles.

Or can she? Setbacks in the form of a tropical storm and its aftermath might not present too great a problem—but when it comes to dealing with an incredibly good-looking plantation owner set on keeping her away from his equally handsome young cousin, what's a girl to do? How can she possibly resist his all-out charm offensive?

There's only one option when temptation arises in Paradise…isn't there?

I hope you enjoy reading my latest book…

With love,

Joanna

HER HOLIDAY MIRACLE

BY
JOANNA NEIL

First published in Great Britain 2016
By Mills & Boon, an imprint of HarperCollins*Publishers*
1 London Bridge Street, London, SE1 9GF

Large Print edition 2016

© 2016 Joanna Neil

ISBN: 978-0-263-26114-1

Our policy is to use papers that are natural, renewable and recyclable products and made from wood grown in sustainable forests. The logging and manufacturing processes conform to the legal environmental regulations of the country of origin.

Printed and bound in Great Britain
by CPI Antony Rowe, Chippenham, Wiltshire

Joanna Neil loves writing romance and has written more than sixty books for Harlequin Mills & Boon. Before her writing career started she had a variety of jobs, which included being a telephonist, a clerk, as well as nursing and work in a hospital pharmacy. She was an infant teacher for a number of years before her love of writing took over. Her hobbies include dressmaking, cooking and gardening.

Books by Joanna Neil

Mills & Boon Medical Romance

Dr Right All Along
Tamed by Her Brooding Boss
His Bride in Paradise
Return of the Rebel Doctor
Sheltered by Her Top-Notch Boss
A Doctor to Remember
Daring to Date Her Boss
Temptation in Paradise
Resisting Her Rebel Doc

Visit the Author Profile page
at millsandboon.co.uk for more titles.

CHAPTER ONE

AT LAST. REBECCA GAVE a soft sigh of relief as a sixty-foot-long catamaran smoothly eased into position alongside the dock. The sound of calypso music came from on board, floating on the air waves towards her, and her spirits lifted in an instant. She'd been patiently standing in the queue for some time, wilting in the heat despite her light camisole top and loose cotton skirt, but now there was an end in sight. She would soon be on the last part of her journey to the beautiful Caribbean island of St Marie-Rose.

Just up ahead of her a man straightened as the boat approached. She'd noticed him earlier—in fact there was no way she could have missed him. He had midnight-black hair and sculpted, lightly tanned features, and he stood out from the crowd—tall, muscular, supremely fit-looking, wearing pale chinos and a white T-shirt that outlined broad shoulders and well-muscled biceps. He'd been looking around, taking in his surroundings. Presently, though, he seemed preoccupied, deep in thought, not at all like the others who lined the quayside.

Perhaps he felt her glance resting on him just then, because he half turned towards her and looked directly at her, his dark gaze meshing with hers for a heart-stopping instant. His eyes widened and his glance moved over her, taking in her slender yet curvaceous figure, the long copper-coloured hair that tumbled past her shoulders in a mass of unruly curls. All at once he seemed stunned, as though he couldn't take his eyes off her.

Heat swept along her cheekbones and she looked away, embarrassed for her own part to have been caught staring. Somehow she hadn't seemed able to help herself…there was just something about him… He probably wasn't a tourist, she decided. There was nothing of the loose-limbed, laid-back sunseeker about him.

Actually, much the same could be said of her right now. She didn't feel at all touristy. After being cooped up in an aeroplane for almost a dozen hours, followed by a short taxi ride to this port, she was more than ready for the last leg of her journey. At least she hoped this was the last leg. It was already late afternoon, and she really wanted to arrive at the house before nightfall. With any luck her sister, Emma, would be there to greet her. She smiled, a thrill of excitement running through her at the prospect—it would be so good to see Emma again.

Up to now, though, nothing had gone quite to plan—instead of flying directly to the island she'd found herself stranded here, on the verdant, equally lovely tropical island of Martinique, waiting for a ferry to take her across the sparkling blue sea to her final destination.

The people in the queue began to move slowly forward. 'Ah, looks like we're boarding at last,' someone said behind her. 'Finally!'

It was a male voice. She turned to glance at him. He was a young man—in his mid-twenties, she guessed, much the same as herself. She was twenty-six. He had blond hair and blue eyes, and a ready smile. Dressed for the heat, he wore three-quarter-length shorts and a T-shirt. Clearly he was in a good mood—most likely returning with his friends from a day trip to Martinique. The three young men with him were chatting to one another, lively and exuberant.

He returned her gaze and waved a hand towards the boat. 'Shall we? I'm William, by the way. William Tempest.'

He looked at her questioningly and she responded in a soft voice, 'Rebecca…Rebecca Flynn…most people call me Becky.'

'Hi, Becky. We should be able to get some refreshments on board. Perhaps I could buy you a drink? I'm not hitting on you,' he hastened to explain. 'Well, maybe I would in different circumstances. It's just that I noticed earlier you were looking a bit fed up and I thought maybe you could do with something to cool you down and perk you up—perhaps an iced juice of some sort—they do a good orange and mango mix?'

'Do they?' So he'd noticed her wilting. What was it that had given her away? Was it her hot cheeks or the way her curls clung damply to her temples? She should have taken the time to pin her hair back while she was on the plane.

She'd no experience of the facilities on board ferries in the Caribbean, but now she moistened her lips with the tip of her tongue in anticipation.

'A cold drink sounds wonderful. I'd like that.' She added as an afterthought, 'This whole thing is a bit of an adventure for me.'

'Are you here on holiday?'

'Sort of. More of an extended break, shall we say? Things were getting me down back home and I needed to get away.'

'Really? I'm sorry. I feel a bit that way, too. I've had a break-up with my girlfriend…it was really hard to take. It was a while ago, and I keep trying to put it all behind me, but it's difficult.'

'Yes. I know how that feels.'

Together, chatting amiably, they walked the short distance along the quay to the boarding ramp and stepped on to the deck of the boat.

It was strange… She didn't know him from Adam, but she liked him instantly, in a platonic, unthreatening kind of way. All her usual English reserve seemed to be disappearing fast—melting away in the tropical sunshine.

Perhaps it was the heady atmosphere of the Caribbean beginning to exert its hold on her— or maybe the energetic beat of the music coming from the boat was serving to loosen her up. Whatever the reason, she'd throw all her inhibitions away right now for the chance of downing a long, cold glass of something. Anything.

William looked around. 'Where do you want to sit? Would you like to be under cover, or do you want to look out over the sea?'

'Both, I think.' She smiled. 'I've been stuck on a plane for several hours, so it will be great to move around and feel the fresh air for a bit.'

He nodded, his mouth curving. 'Sounds great. We can get to know one another—it'll take about an hour to get to St Marie-Rose.'

He was friendly and open with her, and as they

chatted Rebecca was startled to find herself responding readily, a bit like a flower opening up to the sun. Why did she feel so at odds with herself about that? He'd already told her that he was getting over a broken relationship. Would it hurt to talk some more and maybe confide in him in return? He was easygoing and sociable and that was what she needed right now.

'So what's been getting you down?' he asked.

'Oh, a few things…I was ill, and my boyfriend decided that he couldn't handle it.'

'Ouch! That's a tough one. It must have been difficult for you.'

'Yes…'

It had been a few months since her relationship with Drew had disintegrated, and what had happened over that time had certainly taken its toll of her… Complications after her appendicitis had added to her problems and left her feeling low, and Drew had been less than supportive. After her appendix had burst, peritonitis had almost killed her, with the poisons in her bloodstream keeping her in the hospital's Intensive Care Unit for a couple of weeks.

But her problems hadn't ended there. The doctors told her she might be infertile because of the scar tissue from those complications, and that was when Drew had decided to bow out. She had been devastated, overwhelmed by everything that had happened to her. How could she cope with the possibility of never having children? That question haunted her still.

It had all been a bit of a struggle. She desperately needed a change of scene—a chance to put herself back together again. Wasn't it time she tried to relax and let her hair down? It could hardly matter what happened here, what she decided to tell William—he was only going to be around for a short time, after all.

She found a seat on one of the benches under the awning and put her bags down on the floor by her feet while he went to fetch the drinks. Padded bench seats were arranged along the deck, facing a central four-sided counter where dusky-skinned youths were busy cutting up all

manner of fruits—oranges, melons, passion
fruit, limes. There were a couple of urns available for hot drinks, along with juice dispensers
and water coolers. She glanced around. There
were even potted palms placed at discreet intervals on deck, all adding to the holiday atmosphere.

The man she'd seen earlier had gone to stand
by the rail, looking out over the sea. He braced
himself, leaning back against a stanchion, as the
boat's engine started up. He glanced her way,
watching as William came towards her with a
tall glass of iced juice. She couldn't tell what the
man was thinking. His gaze was smoke-dark—
brooding, almost. As though he was disturbed
to see her with another man. That couldn't be
so, though, could it?

For some reason he bothered her. Perhaps it
was because in some way—maybe in the way he
stood apart from the others—he reminded her of
Drew. Though her ex had never possessed those
bone-melting good looks, or that way of looking
at the world as if it was his to command.

'Don't worry about him.' William must have seen her cautious glance, and now, as she accepted the drink he handed her, she looked at him quizzically.

'I won't. Do you know him?'

He nodded. 'He's my cousin. He's been over to Martinique on business—I think he probably wants some space to mull things over.'

'Oh, I see…I think.' She frowned and tried to put the man out of her mind, turning her attention to William and chatting to him about nothing in particular.

He was good company. He was fun and he made her chuckle, and at one point he even pulled her to her feet and had her dancing with him to the hot, rhythmic music that spilled out from the loudspeakers overhead.

Other passengers were already moving to the beat, and from time to time William's friends came to join them. She laughed with them and exchanged banter, simply enjoying the freedom of letting herself go for a while. Her hair tumbled this way and that over her bare shoulders and her skirt gently swirled around her thighs as she sashayed to the beat of steel drums. She hadn't felt this unrestrained in a long time.

The music stopped for a moment as the latest song came to an end and she stood still, attuning herself to the rhythm of the boat as it crested the waves.

'Shall we go and stand by the deck rail for a while?' William suggested, and she nodded, going with him and turning her face to the cooling breeze as the boat ploughed through the waves.

Standing with her by the rail, he put an arm around her shoulders to point out dolphins in the distance, playing in the clear, crystal water.

She felt a prickling at the back of her neck and looked around, suddenly distracted. The man at the rail flicked a glance in her direction, inclining his head in acknowledgement, his eyes narrowed against the glare of the sun. Was he still intent on watching her? Or was it William he was keeping an eye on?

William spoke to her, cutting into her thoughts.

'Perhaps we might see each other again—hang around together from time to time? Don't get me wrong—I know you're not looking for a relationship and neither am I—but we do have something in common. We've both been hurt and we could be friends, maybe?'

'Yes, I'd like that.' It would be good to have a friend out here.

She looked out over the blue water once more. The island of St Marie-Rose was drawing closer, its green-clad mountains beckoning, while picturesque white-painted houses nestled among the trees on the hillsides—a perfect invitation to visit.

'Whereabouts are you staying?' he asked.

'Tamarind Bay. My sister's renting a house there...well, nothing quite so grand as a *house*— it's more of a cabin, really. She was lucky to get it—it's quite secluded, apparently, near to a small private marina. The owner of the property is a friend.'

He frowned. 'That's the opposite direction from me. We're all staying at a rental place in

the north of the island. Still…' He brightened.
'It's not too far away. It's not that big an island.
You could go from one end to the other in two or
three hours.' He smiled. 'There aren't that many
bars and nightclubs in Tamarind Bay. I'm sure
I'll manage to find you again. Maybe I could
have your phone number? I could help cheer
you up.' He made a wry face. 'Heck—we could
cheer each other up.'

She nodded and smiled in response, but she
wasn't about to commit to anything. She wasn't
averse to having fun—in fact it would be great—
but above all she'd come out here to spend time
with Emma.

The catamaran moved into place alongside
the dock at St Marie-Rose just a few minutes
later and they readied themselves to disembark.
Ahead of them, William's cousin was among the
first to leave the boat.

William helped her with her bags as they negotiated the steps to the quay. She paused for a
moment to look around, feeling a deep sense of
satisfaction as she took in the curve of the bay,

with its wide strip of golden sand and palms that tilted towards the sun, their green fronds drifting gently in the light breeze.

'Are you going to be okay getting to your sister's place?' William asked as they stood among the melee of disembarking passengers. 'Tamarind Bay's about an hour's drive south from here.' He seemed concerned, anxious to stay with her, but also aware of his friends waiting for him a short distance away. 'I could find you a taxi. Better still, I could ask my cousin—'

'No, please don't do that,' she said hurriedly. 'Don't worry about me. I'll be absolutely fine. Go and join your mates. Enjoy the rest of your holiday.'

'Okay...' He frowned. 'I suppose so...if you're sure?'

'I am.'

Reluctantly he walked away, and she looked around to see if there were any cabs left for hire. A man thrust a leaflet into her hands—an advertisement for sea trips to the local islands—and she glanced at it briefly. In the meantime passengers were still getting off the ferry, descending upon every waiting vehicle.

'I help you, lady—yes?' A dark-skinned, athletic-looking young man came to stand beside Becky on the dock. 'You need help with your bags?'

'No...no, thank you.' Becky gave him a tentative smile. She'd been warned by the tour company about hustlers, and though he seemed innocent enough she was cautious. Perhaps he had a car somewhere, but from his manner she seriously doubted he was a legitimate cab driver. 'I'll be fine. I'm sure I can manage.'

Unfortunately, her suitcase was still back at the airport, but she had her hand luggage with her—a holdall and a roomy bag.

He shook his head. 'You give me money—I take your bags for you.' He bent down and started to grasp the handles of her overnight bag.

'No, no...please don't do that...I can manage,' she said again, but he wasn't listening.

'I take care of it for you,' he said.

'No—I'd rather you didn't do that.'

She tried to reach for her bag but he was too quick for her, deftly swinging it away from her into the air. She sucked in a sharp breath. How on earth was she going to deal with him? Should she kick up a fuss? Call Security? Where *was* Security around here?

Even as the thoughts darted through her head the man she'd seen earlier stepped forward. He moved so fast she blinked in surprise, watching as he came up to the stranger, gripped the handles of her bag firmly and wrenched them from him. Rebecca was stunned. He was lithe and supple, his body honed to perfection. It was simply amazing to watch him in action.

His steel-grey gaze cut through the young man like a lance. 'She told you that she didn't want your help. Now *I'm* telling you—leave her alone.'

It was clear he meant business. It was there in the clipped tone of his voice and in the firm thrust of his taut, angular jaw. Even Rebecca was in awe of him, and she was an innocent bystander.

'Okay. Okay.' The young man held up his

hands in submission, backing off. 'I didn't mean any harm. I'm going.' He looked wary, taken completely aback by the opposition that seemed to have erupted out of nowhere.

Her rescuer watched him leave. 'He won't bother you any more,' he said.

'No. I see that.' She sent him a grateful glance, her green eyes drinking him in. The youth was hurrying away along the quayside, anxious to stay out of trouble. 'Thank you. I wasn't sure whether there were any security people around here. They didn't seem necessary. Everything looked so peaceful.'

His mouth made a wry curve. 'It is—usually. But anywhere you go you might find people who want to supplement their income any way they can.'

'I suppose so.' She used the leaflet to fan her cheeks against the heat. How did he manage to look so cool and in control? He must be used to the conditions out here.

'I'm Cade, by the way,' he said. 'I'm William's cousin. He may have mentioned me.'

He held out a hand to her and she slipped her palm briefly into his. His grasp was firm and reassuringly strong.

'Rebecca,' she answered. 'Yes, he did. Thanks again for your help.'

'You're welcome.' He gave her a thoughtful look. 'I couldn't help overhearing some of your conversation with William on board. You said you were staying at Tamarind Bay—that's roughly where I'm headed. Near there, anyway. I have a place in the hills above the bay. I could give you a lift, if you like?'

'Um…that's okay, thanks. I don't mind waiting for a taxi. I don't want to put you out.' She didn't know him, after all, so why would she trust her safety to him?

'You could be in for a long wait…' His glance shifted over her. 'To be frank, a woman on her own—a beautiful young woman at that—could invite unwanted attention…as you've already discovered.' He reached into the pocket of his chinos and showed her a business card. 'Perhaps this will help to put your mind at ease.'

Dr Cade Byfield, she read. *Emergency Medi-cine Physician, Mountview Hospital, St Marie-Rose.*

'People know me around here,' he said. 'I make the trip to and from Martinique on a reg-ular basis. Ask the officials at the end of the dock if you need reassurance.'

That sounded reasonable enough. She'd seen one of them acknowledge him with a nod a short time ago. 'A doctor?' she said quietly. 'So you live out here?'

He nodded. 'I have done for the last few years, anyway. I'm from Florida, originally, but my parents settled on the island some years ago.' He glanced at her questioningly. 'And you?'

'I'm English—from a busy town in Hertford-shire.'

'Ah, I thought I recognised the accent.' He smiled fleetingly and waved a hand in the di-rection of the harbour wall. 'My car's parked over there. Shall we go? I promise you, you'll be safe with me.'

'Okay.' As she nodded he placed the palm of

his hand in the small of her back, sending small whorls of sensation eddying through her spine. She tried not to think about the touch of his warm, strong fingers on her body as she walked with him.

'We could have done with your help as a doctor on the plane coming over here,' she murmured as they set off along the quayside.

'Really? Why is that?'

'We had to divert to Martinique to drop off a man who was taken ill. He was sitting in the seat across the aisle from me when he collapsed. He looked dreadful—pale and waxy. The pilot had to radio for help and they made sure they had an ambulance waiting for him at the airport.'

He frowned. 'It must have been serious if they had to do that. What was wrong with him? Do you know?'

She nodded. 'He complained of chest pain radiating to his ears and gums, and then he lost consciousness. I felt for a pulse but there wasn't one.'

He sent her a quick, concerned look. 'Sounds like a heart attack. What happened?'

She pulled a face. 'There was general panic all around me for a moment or two. Then I started chest compressions while a flight attendant rushed to get a portable defibrillator. We managed to shock his heart and establish a rhythm and restored blood flow to his vital organs.' Her mouth flattened. 'I thought he was going to be all right, but then things went wrong again and his heart went into an irregular rhythm and stopped for a second time.'

Cade sucked in his breath. 'He was obviously in a very bad way—that must have been scary for you.'

'It *was* worrying,' she admitted. 'But I'm a doctor, too, so I suppose the training kicked in. They had adrenaline on board in the aircraft's medical kit, so I gave him intravenous doses until he started to recover.'

His eyes widened with interest. 'Are you an emergency doctor?'

'No. My specialty's paediatrics.'

'So, do you work in a hospital or general practice?'

By now they were approaching his car—a dark metallic red sports utility vehicle. It managed to look both sleek and sturdy at the same time, and she guessed it would be capable of managing most types of terrain.

She said quietly, 'I was working in a neonatal unit, but actually I'm taking a break from medicine right now.' How could she bear to go into work every day and be surrounded by babies, knowing she might never hold one of her own? It was like a pain deep inside her. 'At least I thought I was taking a break until I stepped on the plane. My plans certainly went wrong after that.'

He opened the passenger door for her and ushered her inside. He was frowning again. 'Obviously you weren't heading for Martinique at the outset. Wouldn't it have been easier to fly the rest of the way from there instead of getting the ferry?'

'Probably.' She was thankful he hadn't asked

about her reasons for having a break from her career, but maybe he assumed she was just taking a holiday. 'There wasn't another flight until tomorrow morning,' she explained. 'Once we stopped at Martinique the flight crew had worked their allotted hours, apparently. I didn't want to mess about. I wanted to get here on time to be with my sister—and my luggage had already been taken off the plane.' She pulled a face. 'I'm not quite sure where it is at the moment…en route to Barbados, I think. I've filled in all the appropriate forms, so hopefully I'll be reunited with it at some point.'

'You've had an eventful journey.' He slid into the driver's seat and switched on the engine. 'Let's hope things go smoothly for you from now on.'

'Yes, we should look on the bright side, shouldn't we?' She leaned back against the luxurious upholstery and felt the cool waft of a delicate breeze fan her cheeks as the air-conditioning kicked in. 'Oh, that feels good.'

He gave her a sideways glance. 'How long are you planning on staying over here?'

'Three months to begin with—maybe longer, but if so I might need to find work of some sort. I'm not in a hurry to do that yet—I suppose I'm looking for a change of direction. I may even decide to go home when the three months is up. I just want to spend time with Emma—my sister. She's over here on a temporary contract with the nursing directorate.' She frowned. 'She messaged me a short time ago when I was on the boat, to say she'd been called out on a job— some last-minute thing that cropped up. I'm just hoping she'll be back before too long.'

His cool, thoughtful gaze swept over her before he turned his attention back to the road ahead. 'Talking of jobs, it seems a bit strange for you to be taking time out so early in your career. You're very fortunate if you can afford to do that. A lot of people would envy you.'

She winced inwardly. Was that a veiled criticism? After seeing her on the boat, getting on so well with his cousin, he probably thought she was a bored rich girl looking for thrills.

'Perhaps they might. You're right—it's good to have enough money to be able to choose—but I don't see myself as "fortunate", really,' she countered. 'My parents died when I was twelve. They left money in trust for me and my sister, so we're both comfortably off, but I'd much rather they were still around. We were brought up by an aunt and uncle. They've been good to us, but they had their own two little girls to care for. It can't have been easy for them.'

'No, I expect not. I'm sorry.' He studied her briefly. 'Does it bother you, leaving them behind to come here?'

'Oh, yes—I'll miss them all…especially my cousins. But we're all older now, going our separate ways.' She was pensive for a moment or two, lost in thought. 'I suppose we were lucky that there was no rivalry or resentment bubbling away in the background because we were taking up the love and attention that should have been reserved for family. In fact we get on very well with one another. My aunt and uncle did a good job.'

'Four youngsters must have made for quite a lively household?'

'Yes, it was a bit rumbustious at times. We had a lot of fun…holidays and family picnics and generally hanging out together.'

'I never had that experience.' There was a slight thread of regret in his voice. 'I was an only child—that's probably what makes me value my cousin's friendship all the more. We're very close—a bit like brothers.'

She sent him a curious glance. 'Really? I didn't get that impression. You kept to yourself on the ferry and didn't really have any contact with him—he said you'd been to Martinique on business and needed some space.'

'That's right. I had to go over there to talk to some clients—I have a plantation in the hills, a few miles from Tamarind Bay, so I make the journey to Martinique on a fairly regular basis to see people about supplies and exports and so on.'

'Wow!' She smiled. 'I'm impressed…a plantation owner…that's inspiring.'

'Not so much.' His mouth made a wry twist. 'I took it over a couple of years ago, when it was completely run down, and I'm learning a few lessons on the way. It's taking a lot of effort to get it going once more, but we've made a reasonable start, I think.'

'It sounds as though you have a busy life.' She wanted to know more about the plantation, but he hadn't yet commented about leaving his cousin to his own devices. Why had he done that if they were so close? 'You said, "We've made a reasonable start"—is William part of that? Where does he fit in? If you're so close, I don't understand why you didn't want to talk to him on the boat?'

'He works for me, but he's on holiday at the moment. As for when we were on the boat—he was with his friends and I didn't want to intrude…more especially since he seemed to be very taken with *you*. In fact, I'd say he was smitten…so much so that I doubt he'd have thanked me for getting in the way.'

She looked at him in mock surprise. 'Smitten? We'd only just met!' Why would he have reached that conclusion? Was he jealous of the attention William had been giving her? Of course he hadn't heard the bulk of their conversation, or he would have known they were just going to be friends. William liked her, but he was still getting over the break-up with his girlfriend and wasn't making any romantic overtures. 'You're reading too much into the situation.'

'I don't think so.' Again, that wry smile. His glance drifted over her, taking in her slender curves, the way her camisole top nipped in at the waist and her skirt draped itself over the swell of her hips. 'What chance did he have against a flame-haired beauty with emerald-green eyes and a come-hither smile? He was done for the moment he looked at you.' He pulled a face. 'Heaven knows—*I* was done for.'

She stifled an uncertain laugh. Did he really feel that way about her? And that was the second time he'd commented on her looks. 'Well, thanks for the compliment…I think…' He made her sound like some kind of Delilah… 'But if it really was as you say, do you imagine he'd have some sort of a problem getting involved with me? I couldn't help feeling you were keeping a weather eye on him.'

'I was, to be honest.'

She blinked, startled by his frank admission. 'You were?'

He frowned. 'I was…most of the time. At least I was trying to, when I wasn't distracted by thinking about you. There's something about you—a vulnerability that I sensed, maybe. I suppose it must have brought out the protective instinct in me.' He sighed and gave his head a shake, as though he was trying to pull himself together. 'Perhaps William feels it, too. Either way, I don't want to see him land in hot water. My aunt asked me to watch out for him over the next few months. He may not look it, but he's vulnerable, too, right now. He's easily led and he's been hurt in the past.'

'Haven't we all?' She said it under her breath, but he gave her a quick, sharp glance before concentrating on negotiating a twisty bend in the road.

Rebecca gazed out of the window, watching the landscape unfold in all its glory. It was easier than trying to fathom him out. She sensed there was a lot more to Cade Byfield than she'd learned so far. He was attracted to her, but he was fighting it, and at the same time she had a sneaking feeling he didn't trust her around his cousin. She wasn't at all sure why.

Not that it mattered. Did she even trust *herself* right now? She was here to chill out, to get over the breakdown of her relationship with Drew and the turmoil that had caused…and hopefully to recover from the aftermath of the illness that had thrown her life into disarray these last few months.

The road wound its way through forested slopes, and their journey of discovery helped to take her mind off things. Beneath the thick canopy of trees she glimpsed the occasional flight of a colourful parrot or a yellow-chested peewee, and on the ground, which was thickly covered with broad-spanning ferns, she caught sight of small green lizards darting through the undergrowth. There were wild flowers hidden among the foliage along the route—waxy lilac anthuriums and the pretty scarlet rosettes of bromeliads peeking out here and there. It was beautiful, and all new to her.

'You said you often go to Martinique on business?' she murmured, turning her attention back to Cade. 'Wouldn't it be quicker and easier for *you* to fly?'

He nodded. 'That's true. But I like having the chance to unwind on board the ferry. It gives me time to clear my head and maybe get things into perspective. In a place like this you don't always want to be rushing about. I get plenty of that in my job at the hospital.'

He pointed out the pristine waters of a yachting harbour as they rounded a curve in the road. 'We must be getting fairly close to where you'll be staying, I think.'

'Oh…' She gave a small gasp of delight as she looked out over the hillside and down into the rocky cove. 'It's so lovely. It's perfection.' Beyond the shoreline, outlined beneath the deep blue of the sea, she saw the turquoise ridge of a coral reef. 'It's even better than the way Emma described it to me.'

'Yes, it's an exquisite island—a beautiful place to live…and work. I've travelled the world, but I always love to come back here.' He negotiated a winding road down to the scattering of houses that made up the small hamlet. 'Yours is the cabin, you said?'

'Yes…I think I can see it amongst the trees. Emma sent me pictures of it.'

Excitement bubbled up inside her as she caught sight of a timber-clad house with white-framed windows and a white-painted wooden balustrade enclosing a wide veranda. The sun was setting on the horizon, casting a golden glow over the hills as they drew up in front of the house. Everything looked tranquil and untouched by the outside world. She sat for a moment, taking it all in. She could be happy here. She felt it deep inside. Surely this was a place of healing, where she could mend her body and her spirit?

'Presumably your sister would have been expecting you earlier? How will you get into the property if she's not here now?'

She frowned. 'It's been a couple of hours since her text message—I would have thought she'd be home by now. But she said she would leave a key in a safe place where I'd be sure to find it.' She laughed softly. 'Knowing Emma, that probably means it could be under a rock marked *"Key is here".*'

He laughed with her. 'I dare say the locals are all on good terms with your sister. You can rest easy. We don't get a lot of crime out here.'

He parked the car in front of the cabin a few minutes later. It was set against a backcloth of leafy trees and dense shrubbery, its location completely private, and everything smelled fresh and open to nature.

Cade waited while Rebecca knocked on the

door. When there was no answer she stifled her disappointment and went in search of the key.

'It was hidden in a box under the veranda,' she told him. 'Would you like to come in for a drink of some sort? I expect there'll be juice in the fridge—or coffee?'

'Thanks. I'll have a coffee, if you have the makings. I'll see you settled in and then I should be on my way. I have to get over to the plantation to meet up with my estate manager.'

'You work late out here?'

He nodded. 'Occasionally. Sometimes it's necessary if problems crop up. My manager wants to see me about getting a new truck—the one we have at the moment keeps breaking down. He lives in a cottage on the plantation, so it's not as if he'll be put out too much. I need to get it sorted.'

All this on top of his work as a doctor? He obviously believed in keeping busy. She stepped on to the veranda and unlocked the front door. 'Come in.'

'Thanks.'

They both took a moment to look around. The living room was simply furnished, with a polished light oak floor, a couple of settees and a coffee table, and opened out into a light and airy kitchen-diner at one end. The units there were cream-coloured, with pale oak worktops that were easy on the eye. Two sets of French doors led from the kitchen and the living room out on to the veranda that swept around the building, giving a view through the trees of the delightful cove below.

'I'll just see if Emma has any coffee.' Rebecca checked the cupboards, then set out porcelain mugs on the oak table while she waited for the kettle to boil. There was a note from Emma propped up against the sugar bowl. 'She doesn't know when she'll be back,' Rebecca said, quickly scanning it. 'She says the landlord will stop by tomorrow morning to sort out a problem with the window shutters.'

She frowned. It definitely sounded as though she would not be back tonight.

'Ah, I might have known it—Emma's left some

food for supper,' she murmured, continuing to read and then going to rummage in the fridge. 'We might as well help ourselves…there's plenty for both of us, from the looks of things. Spiced chicken drumsticks and salad, with savoury rice.' She turned to him. 'How does that sound?'

He pulled in a breath. 'Too tempting to refuse,' he admitted with a grin. 'It seems to be quite a while since I had lunch.'

'Mmm…me, too,' she agreed, taking dishes and platters from the fridge. She frowned. 'I wish I knew how long she was going to be. I was so looking forward to seeing her again.'

'Is she older than you or younger?' he asked as they sat down to eat a minute or so later.

'Older by just a year. But for all that she's always sort of looked after me…kept me on the straight and narrow, so to speak—our cousins, too. They're three or four years younger than us.' She waved a hand over the food she had set out. 'Help yourself.'

She'd always looked to Emma for guidance over the years. Perhaps Emma would know how she could get over her illness and the break-up with Drew and restore her self-confidence once more. When her consultant had said she might have difficulty in having children because of scar tissue blocking her fallopian tubes it had come as a devastating blow. Rebecca had withdrawn into herself for a while and shut out the outside world. She hadn't wanted to face up to anything for some time.

As for now... A recklessness seemed to have taken her over. She'd left her job, left the country, put everything behind her. And she'd met a handsome young man on the ferry coming over here—not to mention the fact that now she was sharing a meal with a perfect stranger in the privacy of a secluded cabin. Had she lost her senses? Perhaps she was hell bent on self-destruction. She didn't want to take anyone down with her, but was she headed that way? Emma would surely put her right.

She shook the thoughts from her mind. Better to think of something completely different.

'What kind of plantation do you have?' she asked now. 'What do you grow there?'

Cade had been watching her, she realised, clearly curious about her introspection, but now he followed her lead and answered readily. 'Cocoa—everything depends on producing a good crop.'

'You said it had been run down—why would that happen?'

'Because of disease in the plants, the weather—hurricane winds, tropical storms—and low prices. A lot of people out here gave up on cocoa and turned to banana-growing instead. It must have seemed like the better option.'

'But you think you can make a go of it where others have failed?'

He nodded. 'I'll certainly have a good try.' He finished off his chicken and wiped his hands on a paper serviette. 'That was delicious.'

She inclined her head briefly. 'Emma's always been a good cook.'

They talked some more about food in general, and his hopes for the plantation, and then her phone rang, cutting in on their conversation.

'Perhaps it's Emma. I should answer it,' she said quickly.

'Of course. Please—go ahead.'

She stood up and walked across the kitchen to take the call. It wasn't Emma, though, and a swift wave of disappointment washed over her.

'Hi, Becky...it's William. I'm just checking that you managed to get to your sister's all right. I was concerned about you. I hated leaving you alone at the harbour.'

'Oh, hi, William. Yes, I did, thanks. You didn't need to worry about me. I'm fine.' Out of the corner of her vision she saw Cade brace himself slightly. His head went back a fraction.

'That's good. Listen, I'm coming over to the bay tomorrow evening. Maybe we could go for a drink together?'

'I'd like that... It depends what my sister's doing, though. She isn't here right now.'

'She could come with us.'

She thought about it. 'Okay, then. Yes, we could do that. It sounds good. I'll let you know if anything changes.'

'Great. I'll meet you in Selwyn's Bar at around eight o'clock?'

'Selwyn's Bar? Yes. Eight o'clock, then. I'll look forward to it.' She was smiling as she said it, and when she cut the call she turned to look at Cade once more. 'That was your cousin,' she said unnecessarily. 'He was just checking to see that I got here all right.'

'So I gathered.' He stood up, his features guarded. 'You'll be seeing him again, from the sound of things?'

'Looks like it.' She sent him a quick, challenging look. He seemed tense. 'Do you have a problem with that?'

'Not really... Maybe...' He shrugged awkwardly. 'Like I said, I don't want to see him get hurt. He's just come out of a bad relationship and he's vulnerable right now. I know it doesn't seem that way...'

'Surely he's old enough to take care of himself?'

'You'd think so, wouldn't you? But some people take a while longer than others.'

'He seemed fine to me.' Her green eyes flashed. 'Anyway, why do you imagine I'm likely to be such a problem for him?'

'Are you *kidding*?' His mouth made a crooked shape as his glance drifted over her. 'The way you look, I suspect you'd be a problem for a saint,' he said, with feeling. 'My cousin stands no chance at all.'

A wave of heat ran through her cheeks. 'Well, I'm flattered you imagine I have such powers…'

He smiled. 'I suppose I want you to go easy on him. I sense you just want to have a good time and enjoy your stay here—and there's absolutely nothing wrong with that.' His dark eyes glinted. 'I'd be only too happy to help you do that. As for William—he's here for the duration, while you'll be moving on in a short time. I can't help thinking that if you and he get together I'll be left to pick up the pieces again.'

'I'm sure you and your aunt are being overly concerned…I've never thought of myself as a heartbreaker.' Still, something in her prompted her to say, 'Anyway, you could always come with us to the bar.' Even as the words left her lips she wondered what on earth she was thinking. 'He suggested my sister might want to come along,' she added, 'so you could join us and make up a foursome.'

'I'd like that,' he said. 'I'll look forward to it—I'll come and pick you up.' His smoky gaze rested on her once more. 'It's a great pity William saw you first,' he said softly. 'I'd be more than ready for the challenge.'

She looked at him directly, her green glance unwavering. 'I've said before that we're just going to be friends…but even if that wasn't the case I'm not some prize to be won.'

'Like I said, I have his interests at heart. I won't stand by and see him hurt.'

She wasn't sure whether that was a threat or a promise.

He left soon after that, and she watched him drive away. She ought to be feeling relaxed, at peace with herself, but instead she felt a sense of nervous anticipation—a vague worry starting up inside her. What was she doing, getting involved with Cade and his cousin? Hadn't she been through enough turmoil—and could William really get hurt because of *her*?

Her mouth made a crooked twist. She doubted Cade was the kind of man who would let that happen. She frowned. Perhaps that was what bothered her. What did he have in mind? Somehow she suspected a man like him would leave nothing to chance. Wasn't that why he'd been waiting around on the dock after William had left?

CHAPTER TWO

'I WAS SO worried when you didn't come back here last night.' Rebecca watched her sister search through the clothes in her wardrobe. 'Does it happen very often—that you don't manage to get home?'

'Sometimes—it depends on the circumstances.' Emma held up a pale green dress that had an off-the-shoulder neckline and a skater skirt. 'How about this one? It'll go beautifully with your eyes.'

'Oh, that looks great. Thanks. I'll try it on.'

They were getting ready for their night out at Selwyn's Bar, and as most of Rebecca's clothes were still in her suitcase, travelling between airports, she was having to rely on Emma to help her out. Luckily they were of a similar shape and size.

'So what happened last night?'

'We had to go to a rural area up in the hills.' Emma frowned. 'A couple of people have gone down with headaches and fever, and we're not quite sure yet what we're dealing with. We looked after them, made them comfortable, and sent blood samples and so on to the hospital. We shan't know what's wrong with them until we get the results back in a couple of days.'

'So you'll be going back there?'

Emma nodded. 'I have to wait for a call from the chief nursing officer. They'll send a Jeep to take me back to the village.'

The girls finished dressing, and Rebecca added a final touch of blusher to her cheeks just as a rapping noise sounded on the cabin's front door. Her stomach muscles tensed. That would be Cade, of course. He was a few minutes early and she didn't feel at all ready for him. She hadn't had time to compose herself, but she didn't know why that bothered her. Why was she nervous about meeting up with him again?

'I'll get it.'

Her sister left the room and Rebecca took a moment to quickly check her hair in the bedroom mirror. She'd pinned it up for the evening, doing her best to tame the unruly curls, though a few spiralling tendrils had escaped to frame her face. Satisfied that she looked okay, she smoothed down the dress. The silky material skimmed her hips lovingly and fell in soft folds almost to her knees.

Emma was already opening the door, greeting Cade with a cheerful, 'Hi, there. You must be the man Becky's been telling me about. Come in.' There was a pause as he entered the cabin. Then, 'She says you have a plantation up in the hills?' Emma said. 'That is *so* exciting! I've never met an estate owner before—or seen a cocoa plantation.'

'You should come and visit, then,' Cade answered cheerfully. 'I'd love to show you and Rebecca around—you could come tomorrow, if you like?'

'That sounds great.'

'Good. It's a date, then. Late afternoon would

be best for me—I could pick you both up after I leave the hospital.'

'You have to work at the weekend?'

'I do, unfortunately.'

He hadn't wasted any time in issuing the invitation, had he?

His deep voice sent ripples of tingling sensation coursing along Rebecca's spine. She tried to shake it off. How did he manage to have this effect on her? She wasn't looking for any kind of involvement or attachment, yet he'd figured constantly in her thoughts ever since she'd watched him drive away the evening before. It was disturbing. Hanging out with William would be one thing—his cousin was a different matter entirely. With Cade she sensed danger at every turn… Her nervous system had gone into overdrive and was sending out vigorous warning signals that she would ignore at her peril.

'Hello again.' She took a deep breath as she walked into the room, and knew a perverse sense of gratification as she saw Cade's grey eyes widen in appreciation.

He said nothing for a second or two, but then his dark gaze swept over both girls and he commented softly, 'It's clear to see that you're sisters. You have the same high cheekbones and perfect jawline. You both look lovely.'

'Why, thank you!' Emma laughingly touched his arm, her long chestnut hair fleetingly brushing his shoulder as she moved in close to him.

She was wearing a simply styled blue dress with thin shoulder straps, leaving her arms bare. As for Cade, he looked cool and immaculate in a freshly laundered shirt and pale-coloured trousers.

'Just give me a minute to get my bag,' Emma said, 'and we can be on our way. I've been to Selwyn's Bar before,' she confided. 'I love it there.'

Cade led the way to his car a few minutes later and saw them seated comfortably. Rebecca chose to sit in the back seat alongside Emma. It didn't feel as though they'd had much time to talk, since Emma hadn't arrived home until mid-afternoon, and she doubted they'd have much chance to confide in one another this evening. It was good to be together again, though.

'How long have you been working out here, Emma?' Cade asked as he turned the car on to the coast road.

'A couple of months. I'm having a great time out here. The work hasn't been too difficult up to now—mostly we've been running health clinics and visiting the more remote villages. We've been giving vaccinations and checking out the under-fives to make sure they're okay.'

He glanced in the rearview mirror. 'Is that the sort of thing *you* might want to do, Rebecca— work with the under-fives, I mean? Not now, obviously, but maybe later? You talked about wanting a change of direction.'

Rebecca's face paled at the unexpected question. 'Um... I'm not sure. It's something I'd have to think about.'

'I suppose in neonatal your work was much more specialised?'

'Yes. Some of the babies were very ill. They

might have been born prematurely, or they had heart defects or lung complaints and so on.'

'Is that why you stopped doing the job—because it was too harrowing?'

She swallowed hard. 'In a way, yes.'

She didn't want to talk about this. Delving into the different aspects of her work was far too painful, and it brought up a host of reminders she would rather ignore. It had been so hard going back to work after her illness. She hadn't been able to bear to hold those tiny babies in her arms when she might never have one of her own. She hadn't realised how badly she had been affected until she'd cradled those sweet, frail infants.

Beside her, Emma shifted closer in a silent gesture of support. 'Sometimes it's good to do something different for a while—to explore other opportunities. But for the moment Becky's taking time out to recharge her batteries. She's worked really hard over the last few years, qualifying as a doctor and taking her specialist exams.

She hasn't really had much time for herself and she's well overdue for an extended holiday.'

'Of course. I understand.'

Seeing the reflection of his dark eyes in the rearview mirror, Rebecca knew he didn't understand at all. How could he? As far as he was concerned she was young, energetic, on the cusp of life—why would she need to take time out? But she wasn't going to explain her circumstances to someone she'd only just met. And talking about it was upsetting.

She hadn't been able to discuss things much with Drew, because his negative, unhelpful reaction had made matters worse. Whatever future they might have contemplated had been wiped out when he'd realised there was a possibility she might not be able to have children. She'd been devastated by his response to her predicament.

As for now, she wondered if any man she met might respond in the same way? She couldn't even think about her situation without feeling shaky and unhappy. It was too soon…the emotional wound ran too deep and was still too raw.

'They do marvellous mojitos at Selwyn's,' Emma said brightly, changing the subject. 'You'll like them, Becky. They make them with white rum, fresh limes and a sprig of mint. *Yum.*'

'Sounds good.' Rebecca made an effort to pull herself together. She glanced at Cade once more. 'What do you like to drink, Cade?'

'I like rum, too—it's the national drink out here in the islands—but mostly I drink lager. Maybe I'll have a rum cocktail this evening, but after that I'll stick with non-alcoholic lager because I'm on the early shift tomorrow at the hospital… And, of course, I'm driving.'

'Ah…you drew the short straw.' Emma chuckled sympathetically. 'They serve food at Selwyn's, so you could always try soaking up the rum with a tenderloin steak or some such.'

He smiled. 'I might do that.'

William was waiting for them, greeting all three of them with enthusiasm when they stepped on to the boardwalk leading to Selwyn's Bar a few minutes later. The bar was made of wooden decking and built over a shallow tidal strait where mangroves emerged in a dense tangle of arching roots from the flood plain left by the ebb and flow of salt water. There was lush greenery all around, and the sounds of the forest mingled with the lively music coming from speakers positioned under the solid awning. Tables covered in white cloths were set out alongside the balustrade, so that customers could sit and eat and look out over the water.

William was smiling, wearing a T-shirt and knee-length cut-off shorts. 'Hey, it's great to see you again,' he said, giving Rebecca a quick hug and nodding amiably to his cousin. 'And this must be Emma…' He turned to Emma. 'Hi, there. Becky told me you're a nurse? It must be a whole new experience for you to come out here and work in the Caribbean. How are you finding it?'

'It's great…' Emma said. 'It's very different to what I've known before, back in the UK, but it's really good—most of the time. Some things can be a bit frustrating—like equipment shortages or breakdowns—and of course everything tends to move at a slower pace.'

He nodded. 'I know what you mean. Food stores can run out of staples like bread and milk, if you don't get there early in the day, and the Internet can go down when you're in the middle of something.'

'And if your truck breaks down you might have to wait for a part to be sent over from one of the other islands,' Cade put in, with feeling. 'That's happened to us more than once.' He smiled and led them over to the bar. 'I'll get the drinks in. Mojitos, was it?'

'That would be lovely.' Rebecca glanced at him. 'So, did you talk with your estate manager about getting a new truck?'

'I did. It'll take a while to sort out, but things will start to run a lot more smoothly for us once it arrives.'

They took their drinks to a table by the rail and the four of them chatted while they looked at menus and decided what they wanted to eat.

'We could share a seafood and chicken platter?' Cade suggested after a minute or two, and they all agreed. It sounded appetising...saffron rice with grilled spiced chicken and mixed seafood.

Rebecca looked out over the water and watched graceful white egrets searching for titbits in the shallows. In the distance, where the mangroves gave way to tall dogwood trees, she saw a blue-and-gold macaw spread its wings and take flight.

She smiled. 'I love it here,' she said softly. 'It's so restful.'

'It's good to see you looking relaxed,' William commented. 'You were a bit stressed after your journey yesterday.'

Smiling, she said, 'Well, twelve hours on a plane and then finding they've lost your luggage can do that to you.'

Cade lifted a dark brow. 'Have your cases still not caught up with you yet?'

'Not yet. I rang the airport this morning, to check, but nothing doing so far. They don't seem to have any idea where they might be.' Rebecca's mouth curved a fraction. 'It pays to have a sister who'll share her clothes with you.'

'Yeah, I guess so.' He leaned towards her and added quietly, so that only she could hear, 'If that's Emma's dress it certainly suits you…and it fits like a glove.'

Warm colour flooded her cheeks. 'Thanks.'

William was still thinking about the boat journey. 'Actually, I thought there was more to it than lost luggage…there were a few moments when you were off guard and you went a bit quiet.'

'I was fine,' she said. 'I'm still fine. Who could be stressed in a place like this?'

He grinned. 'You're probably right.'

Rebecca sent him a fleeting, thoughtful glance. Was it possible William was more perceptive than she'd given him credit for? Maybe through his own experiences William understood deep down how it was to be out of sync with everything around him and his general air of good humour was something of an effort for him.

She was conscious all the time, though, of

Cade's watchful gaze. He still wasn't happy about her getting to know William to any great extent—she could feel it in her bones—and he'd even managed to arrange the seating at the table so that his cousin was placed next to Emma and sitting diagonally across from Rebecca. Of course that could have come about in the natural course of events—maybe she was reading too much into things.

Cade said now, 'Perhaps you were quiet because you were thinking about that man on the plane—the one who was taken ill?'

'Yes, that was probably it.'

William and Emma listened interestedly as she quickly recounted what had happened.

'That must have been so worrying.' Emma frowned. 'I wonder how he's doing?'

'His condition's stable,' Rebecca said. 'I phoned the hospital this morning. Apparently he's been assessed, and they've made the decision to do heart bypass surgery tomorrow.'

'That must have cheered you up—to know that you enabled that to happen.' Cade smiled. 'It's good that you followed up on him—I was wondering how he was doing, too.'

'From the way the nurse spoke, I'm sure he'll be fine. I think he's in good hands.'

William was momentarily subdued. 'I'm surrounded by medics,' he said, in a voice tinged with awe. 'What *I* do is nothing in comparison.'

'You shouldn't feel that way,' Emma said. 'We all have something to offer.' She studied him briefly. 'You work on Cade's plantation, don't you? What do you do there?'

'I help out in all areas—getting to know the job from the bottom up, so to speak. Cade thinks that's the best way for me to start.'

He told them about his role in ordering new seedlings and supervising the planting.

'When we took over the plantation there were a number of mature trees that were viable—a lot of them are ready for harvesting now,' Cade put in. 'They have to be at least three years old before they produce pods—five years is best for a good crop—but we want to plant seedlings every year to ensure quality and continuity. You'll be able to see what we're doing when you come and take a look around tomorrow.'

'I'll look forward to that,' Rebecca said.

Emma nodded. 'Me, too… Provided I'm not called away to work.' She pulled a face. 'I'd arranged to take a few days off, with Rebecca coming over, but we're not sure if there's some kind of outbreak happening up in the hills.'

A waitress brought their food over to the table and they spent the next hour or so talking about this and that while sampling the delicious dishes on offer. Rebecca ate shrimp sautéed with peppers and onions in a spicy ginger and lime sauce, along with crab cake and rice accompanied by a tasty green salad. Dessert was a delicious concoction of caramelised pineapple with a drizzle of lime, vanilla and rum syrup, and a scoop of ice cream.

'Mmm…that was heavenly,' Rebecca murmured, pushing away her plate when she had eaten her fill. She laid a hand on her stomach. 'I don't think I'll be able to eat another morsel for at least a week!'

William laughed. 'Let's hope it's not as long as that. I was thinking of tempting you with my own recipe for melt-in-the-mouth chocolate tart when you come over to the plantation tomorrow.'

'Oh…chocolate…you've found my weak spot—stay away from me!' She laughed with him. 'So you're planning on being there, too? That's great. But what about your friends on holiday in the north of the island? I thought you would want to be with them?'

'They're going back to Miami,' he said, his mouth turning down a fraction at the corners. 'To go on with their university courses or work commitments. I met them over there, when I was studying food and agricultural sciences, and we stayed in touch after I finished my course. But my vacation ends today, and I'm due back home tomorrow—so, yes, with any luck I'll see you there. I live in one of the cottages on the plantation.'

'That's handy.'

'Yes.' He leaned towards her and spoke confidentially. 'It's rent-free, courtesy of my cousin, so I'm more than happy. I owe him—though he's very dismissive of his generosity.'

Rebecca returned his smile. Cade couldn't hear what they were saying, but all the while she felt his brooding gaze resting on her. He obviously felt great responsibility towards his cousin. She understood his concerns, at least in part, but out-wardly William was fun and that was what she needed right now. She responded to his lively, engaging manner, but it wasn't as if she was set-ting out to capture his heart.

Emma was in a playful mood, too, unwinding after her busy time at work, and was more than ready to let her hair down. She teased William and laughed with Cade.

Both girls drank mojitos, and then at Cade's persuasion Rebecca tried another cocktail, made up of dark rum, lemon juice, grenadine syrup and Angostura bitters. The evening passed quickly and in a bit of a haze after that. She was enjoying herself, but the others had to prepare for work the next day, and so all too soon their night out came to an end.

'I'll drop by the cabin around three-thirty tomorrow, if that's okay?' Cade said as he delivered the girls safely home.

The moon was a silvery orb, glimmering through the branches of the trees, casting shadows all around and highlighting the night-scented jasmine. The heady fragrance of the white flowers lingered on the air.

'Yes, that should be all right. All being well, we'll be ready and waiting.' Emma waved him off as he slid back into the driver's seat of his car and disappeared into the night.

Things didn't turn out quite as they'd expected, though. Rebecca was disappointed when, early the next afternoon, Emma received a text message calling her out to work. Several more people had gone down with the mystery illness in the village high up in the hills, and the nurse in charge wanted extra staff on hand to be available to deal with the ailing patients. They were very ill, apparently, with high temperatures and headaches.

'We think it's some kind of bacterial infection,' Emma told Rebecca. 'We'll probably have to give antibiotics as a precautionary measure.'

'Shall I go with you?' Rebecca asked. 'It sounds as though you could do with some help.'

Emma shook her head. 'No, Becky,' she said firmly. 'You've not long recovered from an illness yourself—you might still be under par and we don't want to risk you going down with anything. Anyway, I doubt the nursing director will allow it.'

'But what about the risk to yourself?' Rebecca was worried, instantly on the alert. 'What if it's typhoid fever? I heard a whisper that there have been sporadic outbreaks on a couple of the other islands.'

Emma shrugged. 'I've had all my vaccinations, so I should be okay. We take precautions, anyway, with gloves and masks where we think it's necessary.'

Rebecca was still anxious, though she stayed quiet, not wanting to upset her sister. The typhoid vaccination wasn't always a hundred per cent reliable—you still had to be careful not to eat or drink contaminated food or water. 'You'll keep in touch, won't you? Phone me and let me know what's happening?'

'Of course I will.' Emma gave Rebecca a hug and then glanced at her watch. 'The Jeep will be here to pick me up in half an hour,' she said. She pulled a face. 'It's such a shame—I was really looking forward to seeing the plantation. You'll have to tell me all about it.'

Rebecca frowned. 'I might ring and cancel… but I'm sure Cade will invite us another time. He and William both seemed keen for us to visit.'

'They did, didn't they?' Emma smiled. 'William's so sweet. He has such an innocent, boyish look about him. He was telling me how much his mother loves chocolate—but she's as thin as a rake, apparently. She's really pleased about him working on the plantation. He's had a bad time lately, from the sound of things…and now his father has been taken ill.'

She hurried away to her bedroom to start packing a few things into a holdall.

Rebecca followed her. She wondered aloud

what was wrong with William's father, but Emma wasn't sure.

'Some sort of virus, I think,' she said. 'They're still trying to figure it out, but it seems to be affecting his heart. It's very worrying, by all accounts.'

No wonder Cade was being protective towards his cousin. It sounded as though he had a lot on his plate right now.

Rebecca searched through one of the cupboards. 'I'll give you a hand. Do you need fresh towels—moisturiser and so on?'

'Yes, thanks.'

Emma left for the village a short time later, and Rebecca tried in vain to phone Cade. Each time she tried she received the unavailable tone. Then, some half an hour later, he knocked on the cabin door.

'Oh, hi,' Rebecca said, trying not to let herself be distracted by his flawlessly turned out appearance. He was wearing a crisply laundered shirt, a pale blue silk tie, and dark trousers that emphasised the tautness of his flat stomach and his powerful, long legs. 'I'm afraid Emma isn't here—she was called away to work. I tried to ring you to cancel, but your phone seemed to be switched off.'

He nodded, frowning. 'I was driving. I tend to switch the car phone off if I'm not on call. Some of the roads in the hills can be tricky—very winding and steep—so I like to give them my full attention, especially if there's been heavy rain or a storm.' He sent her a questioning look. 'I'm sorry she isn't here, but there's no reason for you not to come along, is there?'

'Uh...no...if that's all right with you?' Her brows drew together. 'I know Emma's disappointed to be missing out.'

'It's okay—she can come another time. We'll arrange something. It's no problem.'

She brightened. 'All right, then, if you're sure.' It felt strange to be going without Emma, but since he'd taken the trouble to come out of his way to fetch her, she didn't want to argue the point. 'I'll just get a light jacket.'

A moment later she slipped the jacket on over

her T-shirt, then checked her jeans pocket for her key and cash card, transferring them to a small bag. 'I'm ready,' she said at last.

'Good. I told my manager to expect us just after four. His wife's arranging afternoon tea on the terrace for us.'

'Afternoon tea?' She smiled, giving him a quick glance as she slid into the passenger seat beside him. 'It sounds lovely—but isn't that a very English tradition?'

He smiled. 'It is, but I hoped you might like it. I could certainly do with something—I've been on duty since seven this morning and I'm starving. It isn't always easy to stop and grab something to eat and drink when you're coping with emergencies.'

'No, it isn't.' She recalled her time as a junior doctor, working long hours and fitting in breaks wherever possible. 'Have you been very busy today, then?'

She frowned. He looked clean and fresh after his exertions, but maybe he'd managed to shower and change at the hospital. Come to think of it, his black hair *was* faintly glistening with moisture.

'We have… The usual variety of patients, with chest pains, viruses, bleeding…' He glanced at her, his mouth twisting faintly as he started on the road up into the hills. 'Even though this is the Caribbean, and we have lots of tourists around, enjoying the beaches and water sports quite safely, people still get ill—people who live and work here.'

'I never thought otherwise.' Perhaps he'd mistaken her frown for a look of disbelief that there could ever be trouble in Paradise.

'No?' He didn't say any more, concentrating his attention on the winding road that led ever upwards.

As she gazed out of the window Rebecca saw the cloud-covered peaks of the mountains rising majestically in the distance. The landscape was awe-inspiring, vibrant and rugged.

They arrived at the plantation a few minutes later, and Rebecca looked around in wonder at this dark green jewel set in the midst of the rainforest. All around her were cacao trees, standing about twenty feet high, with glossy green leaves as big as her hand. The tree bark was covered with mosses and lichens, and small, delicate orchids peeped out from crevices here and there. Large pink fruit pods hung from the branches, ready to be harvested.

Set amongst these trees were other, taller ones. She recognised banana and coconut palms. She looked at them, a little puzzled, wondering what they were doing here in the middle of a cocoa plantation.

Interpreting her glance, Cade said, 'They provide shade for the cacao—otherwise the hot sun would shrivel them. The cocoa trees are quite fragile, especially when they're young, so they need protection. I planted these trees when I first took over the plantation so that I could shield the young plants. They grew very quickly.'

'Ah, I see.' The banana leaves were huge, spreading shade, and the nearby coconut palms added extra security.

'Up ahead they're harvesting the pods—we can go and watch for a while, if you want?'

'I'd like that—thanks.'

She went with him to an area where workers moved among the more mature trees, hooking the pods from the branches with long-handled implements. The pods fell to the ground, where young men and women with machetes cut them open and removed the white beans from inside. They dropped the large seeds into clean metal buckets.

'They'll empty the beans into wooden boxes and cover them with banana leaves to keep in the heat,' Cade told her. 'We let them ferment for a few days before drying them, so that the colour and flavour can develop.'

'It's fascinating,' she said simply. 'I'd no idea the beans were white to begin with.'

His mobile phone pinged and he took it from his pocket and glanced at a text message on the screen. 'If you're interested I can show you more of the process,' he said, 'but maybe we should go and have tea first. It's all ready and waiting for us at the house, apparently.'

'Okay.' She smiled and started to walk with him towards the white-painted building in the distance. 'Is William there? I was expecting to see him this afternoon.'

A muscle flicked briefly in his jaw. 'Actually, no… Perhaps I should have mentioned it earlier…I'm afraid William won't be back until much later today—he's gone to a neighbouring island to organise the transportation of our new truck. Things will go a lot quicker for us if he takes charge of it, I think.'

She shot him a quick, penetrating glance. 'You sent him to do that today?'

He nodded. 'The dealer called this morning. It seemed to me like a good opportunity to follow up on things right away.'

He sounded nonchalant, though she suspected he was covering his actions. The truth was he hadn't wanted her spending more time around his cousin.

'Really?' She eyed him doubtfully.

Had it been so necessary for William to go this afternoon? Wouldn't a phone call have been enough to set things in motion? She frowned. It wasn't up to her to interfere, or tell him his business, but she was suddenly on edge, wary of Cade's motives. Did he think she was such a bad influence?

'It's a shame he isn't here,' she said. 'I know he was looking forward to seeing Emma and me today.'

His dark eyes glinted in a way that only confirmed her suspicions. He'd deliberately sent his cousin on this errand.

'I'm sure he was, but I dare say there'll be other opportunities for you to get together.'

He laid a hand lightly in the small of her back, and with that gentle possessive touch it dawned on her that maybe he wanted to keep her all to himself. His dark gaze moved over her and a small ripple of panic ran through her—a feeling of nervousness mingled with a strange sadness. She couldn't get involved with anyone, could she? Any relationships she had from now on would have to be light-hearted, fleeting—nothing of any great significance. She didn't want to risk getting the same reaction she'd had from Drew. Once had been quite enough.

They'd arrived at the plantation house by now, and were standing in front of wide veranda steps. It was a beautiful house, built of stone to withstand the ravages of Caribbean storms, and meant to last a lifetime. There were lots of glass doors opening out on to the decking, giving her a glimpse of a light and airy interior.

Just then a woman came hurrying from the house. She was in her mid-forties, Rebecca guessed, with neat brown hair cut into a silky layered bob, and hazel eyes that were filled with anxiety.

'Cade—there's been an accident in the east section. One of the lads has hurt his hand—a machete cut. Don says it's bleeding quite badly.'

'Thanks, Harriet,' he said, looking worried. 'I'll go and get my medical bag.' He glanced at Rebecca as he moved towards the house. 'I'm afraid I'll have to go and deal with this right away. Will you stay here and let Harriet look after you? I'll be back as soon as I can.'

'It's all right. I understand—you have to go, of course.'

All her instincts as a doctor kicked in as soon as she realised that this was an emergency. If the cut had gone deep the boy would need stitches at the very least. If there had been major damage to the muscles and tendons of his hand he might require an operation in order to save the function. There was also the possibility that Cade might need help with administering an anaesthetic...

Deep down, she knew she didn't have a choice. 'Perhaps I should go with you to see him?'

He didn't argue the point. 'Are you sure you want to do that?' He raised questioning dark brows, and when she nodded said, 'Thanks. We'll take the runabout.' He pointed to an open-sided vehicle parked on the drive. 'It'll get us there in a few minutes.'

He went into the house and came out a minute later with a large immediate care response pack.

She was impressed. 'It looks as though you're

very well prepared for any eventuality,' she commented, as they climbed aboard the four-seater golf buggy and set off.

He nodded. 'I always keep a medical kit in the car, too. I'm on call outside the hospital sometimes, so I need to be ready for anything.'

'I can understand that.' A worrying thought occurred to her. 'Does this sort of thing happen often here on the plantation?'

'No, not at all. We're really careful to show our workers the correct way of going on, but I suppose it's inevitable that accidents happen from time to time. The aim is to keep them to a minimum.' He frowned. 'One way I've changed things is by paying everyone a proper wage, instead of giving payment for how much they produce. It seems to be working out for the better so far.'

They arrived at the east section a short time later, and he jumped down from the runabout and hurried over to where a small crowd of native workers had gathered. There were murmurs of concern, people talking all at once, but as soon as Cade appeared the group quietened and opened up to give him access to his patient.

He knelt down beside the injured boy, a lad of about seventeen years old. He was holding his hand to stem the blood flow, his face etched with pain. He was pale and in shock.

'Let me see, Thomas.' Cade examined the wound—a deep cut across the back of the hand between the thumb and first finger. 'Can you move your fingers? Open and close your hand for me?'

After examining him carefully, Cade gave an almost imperceptible nod.

'I think you're fortunate—there's been no major damage. You've lost quite a bit of blood, and obviously you're in shock. I think we'll need to clean up the wound and put in a few stitches.' He studied the boy thoughtfully. 'I could take you to the hospital, or we could do it back at the house. What would you prefer?'

'Will you do it here…please?'

'Okay.' Cade rummaged in his medical bag and brought out a pack of sterile dressings. 'I'm going to put a pad over the wound to stem the bleeding and then cover it with a dressing. Once we get you to the house we'll clean it up properly and put some sutures in place.'

All the while he was speaking, he was working efficiently to protect the injured hand.

'Okay, let's get you into the runabout.' He signalled to two of the workers to help get the boy settled in the back of the buggy. 'How did you come to hurt yourself, Thomas, do you know?'

Thomas shook his head. 'It happened so suddenly...I was cutting open a pod with my machete and I saw something out of the corner of my eye—it might have been a small lizard, running through the undergrowth.'

'Hmm...that's a difficult one. These things happen sometimes, but you need to try to keep your attention on the blade at all times.' Cade frowned. 'Maybe we should issue everyone with leather gloves?'

'Too hot, boss,' one of the workers said. 'No one would want to wear them.'

'Well, we'll have to think of something—

maybe we can find gloves that have air holes…
I don't want any more accidents if I can help
it.' He glanced at the other worker once more.
'Benjamin, will you make sure Thomas's parents
know what's happened? Tell them he'll be okay.'

'I will, boss.'

Cade nodded, and saw the boy settled into the
buggy while Rebecca slid into the seat beside
the patient, making sure that he was securely
strapped in and that his arm was supported in a
comfortable position.

Back at the house, Cade helped Thomas
through the front door and into a room that
seemed to serve as a clinic. Rebecca looked
around, taking in the clean lines, the treatment
couch laid with fresh tissue roll, the glass-fronted
cupboards stocked with all kinds of medical supplies. In one corner there was a sink unit with
stainless-steel taps and dispensers for soap and
paper towels.

'Sit down here, Thomas. Let me adjust the
backrest for you.' Cade settled the boy on the

couch and then went over to the sink to wash his hands.

Rebecca joined him there. 'Do you want me to help anaesthetise the hand?' she asked, and he nodded.

'Thanks. We'll use lidocaine, and then clean the wound with sterile water. He'll need several stitches to hold it in place.'

She worked with him to tend the boy's injured hand, and when Cade had finished applying the sutures she covered the wound with a sterile dressing, fixing it in place with tape.

'I'll give you some antibiotics, Thomas,' Cade said, 'so that you don't get an infection. It's important to keep the wound clean, okay? I'll need to see you back here in a week's time, to check that everything's healing as it should.' He looked at the boy carefully. 'Are you okay with that?'

Thomas nodded. 'Yes, thanks.' He was still pale, but at least he appeared to be recovering from the initial shock of the accident.

'Mrs Chalmers will give you tea and something to eat in the kitchen,' Cade said, helping him to get down from the couch. 'Take your time—your father will be along in a while to take you home, but there's no rush.'

Thomas smiled. 'Thanks, Dr Byfield. I'm sorry to be so much trouble.'

'You're no trouble, Thomas. I don't like to see anyone injured—especially on my property. I want you to take extra-special care from now on.'

'I will. Thanks again.'

Cade took him along to the kitchen—a large, superbly equipped room with doors that opened out on to a wide area of the veranda. A table and chairs were set out there, and Harriet Chalmers was waiting with reviving tea, home-baked scones and fruit preserves.

Thomas's father arrived just as the boy began to tuck in, using his good hand, and Cade spoke to the man for a few minutes, inviting him to sit down and eat with his son before turning his attention back to Rebecca.

'We'll leave them to it,' he said. 'Harriet's set

out some sandwiches for us in the breakfast room—through here.'

He led the way from the kitchen to a small room, surrounded on two sides by floor-to-ceiling glass doors. It was simply furnished, with a white table and chairs, and a white-painted dresser displaying plates and dishes that added a pleasing splash of colour. Here and there were green ferns, extending their delicate fronds to bring a touch of the outside into the room.

An arrangement of pale yellow orchids on the breakfast table caught Rebecca's attention and she gave a small gasp of delight. 'Aren't they beautiful?' she said, smiling. 'This room is lovely. It's so cool and fresh and restful.'

'I'm glad you like it.' Cade returned the smile and pulled out a chair for her. 'Harriet fetches the flowers from the garden. She looks after the house for me and prepares food—she thinks I'll starve if I'm left to my own devices.' He thought about that for a moment or two, a small line furrowing his brow. 'Actually, she's probably right about that. I've never been any good at cooking—apart from eggs or pancakes.'

'You're lucky to have her, then.'

She looked at the array of food that had been set out. There were perfectly cut triangular-shaped sandwiches arranged on a platter, decorated with a crisp-looking side salad. Alongside that were skillets filled with chicken kebabs made with peppers and mushroom, bowls with savoury rice, and a mango salsa dip.

'Oh, what I would give for someone to cook for *me*! Beyond price!'

They ate the food, drank hot tea and talked about Cade's hopes for the plantation.

'Did you start all this with William in mind?' she asked after a while. 'It must have seemed relevant that he was studying food and agricultural science at university.'

He nodded. 'That did come into it,' he admitted. 'But my father was always interested in growing food, so I suppose I developed an interest along the way.'

'What does he do? Does he have some sort of

farm or plantation? Or work on one?' She wondered why he didn't work with his father if they shared the same passions.

'He lives back in Florida now, and works on one of the teams doing restoration work in the Everglades. His interests have changed over the years.'

His tone was faintly cynical and she immediately picked up on that. Was there some kind of problem between him and his father?

'Do you see much of him? It must be difficult for you…working at the hospital *and* running the plantation.'

'We keep in touch. I see him at least once a month—but when he and my mother split up my priority was to make sure *she* was all right.'

'Oh, I'm sorry. I didn't realise—does your mother live on the island?'

'She does.' He smiled. 'She was part of the inspiration behind the cocoa plantation—she and her sister…William's mother. They're both hugely interested in how it will turn out. She lives fairly close—just a mile or so away—so I see her often.'

'That's good. Family's important.'

'Yes. You tend to find that out when you don't have it—as you know. I guess we've both lost out, though in different ways.' He sent her a penetrating glance. 'It must be disruptive for you, with Emma being called away? All your plans for doing stuff together must have been put on hold for the time being?'

'Yes.' Her mouth flattened. 'It's a bit of a blow, but it can't be helped. I'll probably take the time to go and look around the island. From what William told me there are lots of places to see, beaches to lie on, markets to visit. I'd like to see the other islands at some point, but I suppose I've plenty of time to do that with Emma.'

'Well, yes, from the sound of things you'll be here for a few months, so there should be plenty of opportunity for you to explore.' He looked at her oddly. 'I guess it's great to get the chance to take time out from your career.' He frowned. 'Though from what I saw this afternoon when you helped with Thomas, the way you talked to him, and from what happened on your plane over here, you're a highly skilled, competent physician. It seems strange that you've put it all on hold to come halfway around the world.'

'Does it?' She picked up her cup and drank slowly. 'You're quite right—people don't often get the chance to do that, do they? Maybe I'm just taking advantage of my special circumstances and making the most of things.' She spoke nonchalantly, as though it didn't matter one way or the other, but as she viewed him over the rim of her cup she knew he didn't accept her answer.

'Did something happen, back in Hertfordshire?' he asked. 'Something that sent you on the run?'

She hesitated for a second or two. Then, 'Nothing that I want to talk about,' she said flatly.

He pulled in a quick breath. 'I'm sorry. I shouldn't have pried.'

'It's okay.' She glanced at her watch. 'It's getting late. Perhaps I should call for a taxi to take me home. I've taken up enough of your time.'

'Not at all…I have to stay here to supervise the workers, but I'll arrange for Benjamin to take you home. I'm glad you came along this afternoon. Maybe we could meet up for a drink this evening?'

She shook her head. 'I'm sorry, but I'm afraid I've already made plans.'

He frowned. 'With William?'

'With a friend of Emma's.'

'Oh, I see.' He relaxed a little. 'Is she one of Emma's nursing colleagues?'

'No—actually, he's Emma's landlord. He dropped by earlier today, to check that everything was okay with the property, and after we'd talked for a bit he asked me out. I thought, why not? Since Emma isn't going to be around.' She paused momentarily, sensing Cade's sudden tension in the bracing of his shoulders and the narrowing of his eyes. She sent him a quick glance from under her lashes. 'I suppose that only confirms your opinion of me as some kind of good-time girl?'

He returned her gaze with penetrating scrutiny. 'Oh, I don't know about that, Rebecca. You seem to be intent on enjoying your stay out here in the Caribbean—good luck to you in that. I'd be only too glad to help you make the most of your stay on the island in any way I can.' He frowned. 'I can't help thinking, though, that there's a whole lot more to you than meets the eye…I guess I'll just have to bide my time and look forward to getting to know you better.'

CHAPTER THREE

REBECCA LISTENED TO the wind howling about the cabin and shivered unconsciously. Already it had whipped up trouble and blown down a fencepost. It could be that a freak tropical storm was threatening but, whatever the situation, she had to go outside and fix the post before the whole fence collapsed.

The weather had changed overnight, and she wasn't sure what to make of it. It was definitely a bit scary…though she doubted she'd be worried about it if Cade were there with her. Somehow with him around she was fairly certain she would feel safe and secure. But he wasn't here. Nor was he likely to be.

She hadn't known what to make of his comments the other night. She'd tried to keep her feelings hidden deep inside herself, but it looked as though he'd guessed she was holding something back.

Now, as she went outside, she wondered what made him tick. He was obviously a perceptive, ambitious, intelligent man, who cared deeply for the people around him. He even knew the names of all his workers—that had surprised her, because she'd seen for herself that there were a good many of them employed on the plantation, but in a moment alone with the housekeeper Harriet had confirmed he knew every one. From other things he'd said, he knew their families, too, and about their hopes and their worries.

She straightened the wooden post in the ground and hit it squarely with a mallet she'd found in the outhouse, but her efforts didn't appear to be having much impact. It still remained stubbornly loose and tipped over to one side.

'Try holding the mallet further back along the handle. It'll give you more leverage.'

Startled, she looked up to see Cade standing by the wide-spreading fig tree. Its glossy leaves lifted fitfully in the breeze and sent dappled shade over the garden. 'Cade,' she said in surprise. 'Hello.'

He looked incredibly good, dressed in a dark, beautifully tailored suit, his jacket open to reveal a pale blue shirt and deeper blue tie.

'I didn't hear you arrive. Is everything okay? I wasn't expecting to see you.' Her copper curls flicked about her face and she pushed them away with the back of her hand.

'I was coming home from the hospital and I thought I'd drop by to see how you were doing. I've been on call or I'd have come sooner. It's been a couple of days since you were up at the plantation, hasn't it?'

'Yes... Though I saw William yesterday. He's been keeping me up to date with things. He said he'd brought the truck over and everything is going well with the harvesting—and that Thomas wants to be back at work but you think he should wait until the stitches are removed.'

She wielded the mallet once more and this time the post sank a few centimetres into the ground. It was still not enough, though, and she stared at it in frustration. She wasn't making much headway. The wind had done a good job in dislodging the post and tipping over the fence—even now it was buffeting around her, promising mayhem.

He reached for the mallet. 'May I?' he said, and she nodded, handing it over. He hammered the post effortlessly into place with a couple of hefty swings. 'Shouldn't your landlord be doing these repairs for you?' he asked, attempting to straighten the rest of the fence slats and fixing them to the main post with the nails she handed to him.

She shrugged, causing her loose-fitting top to slide downwards, leaving a shoulder bare. 'It was hardly worth fetching him out for such a minor thing—though I'm sure he would have obliged if necessary.'

His glance moved over the smooth expanse of creamy flesh exposed inadvertently and her cheeks flushed with heat.

'I've no doubt you're right,' he said, 'but I hope he fixed the window shutters for you—there's a

storm brewing and you'll need to be able to bat-
ten things down.'

'Yes, he did. It was something simple—a couple of rivets missing. It wasn't worth bringing a
workman in to do it, he said. He did the repair
himself.'

'I'm glad that's sorted. That's partly why I
came over here—to make sure you were all right
and prepared for the weather.' He hammered a
nail home and then studied her thoughtfully. 'So
how did your date with him go?'

'It went well, actually,' she said brightly.

It was somehow good to know that Cade cared
about her enough to check that she was okay…
but perhaps she ought to remain cautious in her
dealings with him. It might be just as well if he
realised she wasn't confining her attention to
William, considering he seemed to have such a
problem with that—even though 'that' was just
friendship! She wasn't sure what she wanted in
the love department any more…

'He's surprisingly young for a landlord—in his
early thirties,' she said. 'But I guess it's a family-

run enterprise. His parents are in business over here, dealing in property. He showed me round some of the houses they own and then took me to a nightclub in a resort along the coast. We had a great time.'

His eyes narrowed. He didn't seem too happy with her answer. 'Are you going to be seeing him again?'

'Possibly.' She'd enjoyed her evening with him, and they'd met up for coffee the next day, but when he would have taken things further she'd held back, doubts creeping in. He was keen, but she wasn't ready for that level of involvement. 'We exchanged phone numbers, but I'm a bit cautious about making too many arrangements until I know when Emma's going to be coming back. I don't want her returning to an empty house.'

'I suppose that's understandable.' His shoulders relaxed a bit. 'Have you heard anything from her? William told me you were getting anxious. She's been gone for a couple of days now, hasn't she? Though that's probably to be expected if there's an outbreak of some sort?'

Finishing up, and checking the fence was secure, he returned the mallet to her.

'Thanks.' She nodded agreement. 'I think there must be something wrong with the phones—a problem with the signal up there in the hills, or some such. She promised she would call me, but perhaps there was a local storm. Otherwise I'm sure she would have been in touch. It's a bit of a worry.' She put the mallet into the storage shed and padlocked the door. 'Shall we go into the house?'

'Good idea—we definitely need to get out of this wind. I just need to fetch something from my car—I have your luggage in the boot, courtesy of the airline authorities.'

She stared at him, her eyes widening in astonishment. 'You *do*?'

He nodded. 'I gave them a call and chased things up, since you weren't having much success… William mentioned it still hadn't turned up. I hope that's all right with you? My handling things? I've had more dealings with people out here...'

'All right? *Definitely* it's all right. You tracked it down? Oh, that's wonderful! I was beginning to think it was gone for ever! How on earth did you manage it?'

He made a crooked smile. 'It was a process of elimination—tracing the route it was most likely to have followed, starting with the trip to Barbados, then back to Martinique. It did a bit of a detour along the way, but I got them to forward it here.'

'Bless you for that. Oh, *wow*!' She wanted to hug him, but contented herself with touching his arm in a brief show of gratitude. They walked around to the front of the house and she watched as he lifted her cases from his SUV. 'Bring them inside, will you? Thanks. Oh, it's *so* good to have them back!'

'I thought you'd be pleased.' He looked around as he stepped into the cabin. 'Where do you want them? In your bedroom?'

'Yes, please—it's through here.' She showed him the way to the second bedroom.

He glanced at the neatly made bed with its mosquito net drapes and then at the desk with her laptop computer set up in a corner of the room. There were doors leading on to the veranda.

'Your sister did well to find this place,' he said, placing the cases at the end of the bed. 'It seems to have everything going for it.' He straightened and looked around properly.

He was very tall, very muscular—an overwhelming male presence in the confines of the small room.

'It does.' She moved to the door, suddenly very much aware of him and a little uncomfortable to be standing in a bedroom with him. 'Come through to the kitchen. I'll make us some coffee.'

'That would be great, thanks.' He went with her and helped set out mugs, cream and sugar on the table, while she added freshly ground coffee to the filter machine and searched for cookies in the cupboard.

'These are made with cinnamon,' she said, opening a packet and sliding them on to a plate, pushing it towards him. 'I found them in the bakery in the village. Help yourself. They're delicious.'

'Thanks.' He took off his jacket, draping it over the back of a chair, and waited while she poured coffee. Then he sat down with her at the table.

'Do you really think there's a storm coming?' she asked. She sipped the hot liquid.

'I'd say it's practically on top of us,' he said. 'It's already affected the south part of the island and it's moving towards us all the time. The wind's building up and it won't be too long before the rain starts.'

She bit her lip. 'Perhaps I shouldn't be keeping you here—you still have to drive up into the hills. I'm not sure what to expect, but from what I've been hearing on the radio these things are a lot more powerful than the storms we get back in England.'

'Are you worried about that?'

'I'm not sure. I suppose so… It's the not knowing that's the worry.'

'I could stay with you—we can see it out together?'

He glanced at her and she gave an almost imperceptible nod, relief flooding through her.

'Would you? I think that would make me feel much better.'

'Of course.' He drank his coffee and then headed purposefully towards the door. 'First thing to do is to close the shutters,' he said. 'It'll make things dark in here, so you might want to put on the lights and check if you have any candles.'

'Do you think the power might fail?'

'It could do. It often happens—lines come down…services get disrupted. You get used to it after a while. The water sometimes goes off as well, so it might be useful to fill some containers as a precaution.'

He went outside and started closing the shutters. As he'd said, it became dark in the house once the doors and windows were blacked out, and he finished the task only just in time as the first drops of rain started to fall. It very soon became pounding, torrential rain.

She looked outside as he came back in through the kitchen door and the sky was ominously dark, with storm clouds gathered overhead. He shut the door behind him and she busied herself pouring more coffee and listening to the reports on the radio.

'They say it's heading north towards the other islands,' she said. 'I hope Emma and her colleagues are okay.'

He frowned. 'I expect they'll be fine away from the coast. Situated here, by the sea, we're probably bearing the brunt of it.'

Thunder boomed overhead, shaking the cabin, and her eyes widened in dismay. She tried to ignore the tumult outside, talking to him about anything and everything—about the beautiful Caribbean islands and beach barbecues, the colourful wildlife that lived in the trees around the cabin—and he told her about his work at the hospital, how he'd come to medicine through his interest in the work of the doctors back in Florida, where he'd grown up.

As the day wore on flashes like strobe lightning sparked through the gaps in the shutters and the wind screamed around the cabin. This was nothing like the mild storms she'd experienced back home. This was violent, booming, nature at its most destructive.

'It'll be okay. It sounds worse than it really is.'

'If you say so. It's been going on for hours.' She went over to the stove. She needed to keep busy. 'It's getting late,' she said. 'I could make us some soup, and there are some crusty rolls and butter we can have with it.'

'That sounds great.'

Another thunderclap shook the cabin and there was an almighty rumble overhead, followed by a shrill clattering on the roof. She jumped slightly and felt the colour drain from her face. It seemed as though the very fabric of the house was being torn apart.

Cade came over to her and put his arms around her, holding her close. 'We'll be all right,' he reassured her. 'It was probably just a few loose shingles on the roof. This place is solidly built.'

She nodded, knowing he was doing his best to comfort her. It was soothing, having him draw her to him this way. He wasn't at all bothered by the hurricane force that hurled itself in a fury around the building. That knowledge in itself was calming, and she leaned into him, gaining strength from him, glad of the steady thud of his heartbeat beneath her breast. His powerful body shielded her, offered protection while the storm raged around them. She was ashamed of herself for needing that comforting gesture, but all the time she was thankful that he steadfastly held her.

Even so, there was another inherent danger in being in close proximity to him in this way. She was becoming far too aware of him—of his strength, his lithe, supple body, the way the lightest touch of his hands evoked a tingling response.

'I think I'll be okay now,' she said after a while. She couldn't let him go on supporting her this way. It was too intimate, too tempting to stay here, locked in his embrace. If this carried on she might want to make a habit of it—and that wouldn't do at all, would it?

'Are you sure?' He looked at her, his gaze smoke-dark as he tried to read what was in her mind. 'I promise you I'm quite happy to go on holding you for as long as you like.'

Heat flickered in his grey eyes and a half-smile pulled at the corners of his mouth. She was feverishly conscious of the warmth of his body, the taut muscles of his thighs pressuring hers, of the way his long body offered refuge.

'I'm sure. I'll be fine.' She couldn't allow herself to respond to his mischievous invitation. Instead she carefully began to ease herself away from him, and in the end he reluctantly let her go. 'I'll…I'll see to the soup,' she said.

He watched her as she worked. 'Did you have a boyfriend back in Hertfordshire?' he asked. 'I can't imagine a girl like you not being scooped up by some determined man. Have you left someone behind—someone who's nursing a bro-ken heart, maybe?'

She gave a small choked laugh at that. Even now it brought a lump to her throat to think about Drew. She didn't have feelings for him any more, but the hurt and associated fall-out from their relationship still lingered.

'There was someone, but it didn't work out,' she said. 'You could say I've decided to move on.'

'Ah.' He was silent for a moment, his glance drifting over her. 'I thought there had to be something like that.'

She stirred the soup and set out bowls on the table. 'What about you?' she asked. 'You have everything going for you, but I don't see a woman around.'

His mouth flattened a little. 'Perhaps I've learned to be cautious over the years. Women tend to come with their own agendas, I've found... They want marriage, wealth, status—all perfectly reasonable ambitions, but no good if they come at the expense of true, basic human feelings.'

'So you've been hurt? Someone let you down?' She said it in a matter-of-fact way, glancing at him as she served up the hot vegetable broth. 'Just because you've had one or two bad experiences it doesn't necessarily mean that *all* women think along those lines.'

He shrugged. 'Maybe not.'

He wasn't convinced of that, obviously. 'Is that why you're so concerned about William—you think he might be hurt in a similar way?'

'In part. He fell for someone, but she led him a bit of a dance and cheated on him. He was heartbroken. Then his father was taken ill, and he became the main breadwinner in his household, and things became too much for him for a while.'

She frowned. 'And now?'

'Now he seems to be coping well enough. My uncle's in hospital, being treated for a virus that has affected his heart muscle. They had to sell the house to fund the medical bills, and now they live in a property on the plantation. It's made me all the more anxious to make a success of things, so that I can give them a livelihood. William will become a partner one day, and maybe my uncle, too.'

So there was more than his own land-owning expectations resting on the venture. 'I'm sorry for what you're all going through.' She sucked in a breath. 'Is your uncle going to be all right?'

He pulled a face. 'We hope so. The doctors are giving him supportive treatment, along with a low-salt diet, and they're making sure he gets plenty of rest. It all depends on how serious the damage is and whether his heart can recover from it.'

'I'd no idea it was so bad. William manages to hide his feelings well, doesn't he?'

'He does.'

They sat at the kitchen table, savouring the food, and by mutual unspoken agreement changed the subject, talking about how the storm might affect the plantation.

'It's possible we could lose a few trees,' he

said. 'But the main harvest is in, and in general the crop and the houses are protected, so things may not be too bad. The biggest worry is the road network. Rivers tend to swell and flood, and you often find that debris is swept along in their path.' His phone bleeped but he ignored it, going on with his soup.

'I imagine the authorities are used to dealing with—' She broke off as another thunderclap exploded in the distance and all the lights went out. 'Oh, no…there goes the power.'

He stood up and went over to the worktop, where she'd set out hurricane lamps and candles. 'Good—these are battery-operated,' he said, bringing one of the lamps over to the table. It gave out a decent light, so they were able to finish their meal in relative comfort.

When she started to clear the table a little while later she was suddenly aware of the gentle splash of water droplets dampening her hair and her clothes. 'Oh, dear…' She glanced upwards, searching for the source, and discovered a dark patch of moisture spreading across the ceiling.

'I guess I was right about the shingles on the roof,' Cade said, making a wry face. 'There must be a tear in the roofing felt. I'd better do a quick check on the rest of the house.'

He took one of the hurricane lamps with him and went from room to room, searching for more seepage. Rebecca went with him, dismayed to see similar patches of water forming on her bedroom ceiling.

'I'll do what I can to stop the leaks temporarily,' Cade said, 'but your landlord will have to get things fixed as soon as he gets the chance.'

'I'll let him know. Is there anything I can do to help?'

'You could see if there are any sheets of polythene or something similar that I can use to mask the tears,' he suggested.

'Will bin liners do?'

'They'll be fine. I could do with some tape, as well.'

She searched in one of the kitchen drawers and pulled out a roll of plastic liners, handing them to him. 'I think we have some PVC tape in a toolbox in the loft. I'll get it for you—the loft access is in the hallway. There's a pull-down ladder.'

'Okay, leave it with me.'

She didn't leave him. Instead she stood at the foot of the ladder and held a second lamp to give him more light as he accessed the roof space. It took several minutes for him to locate the leaks and fix the waterproof sheeting in place, but finally he came back down the ladder to her.

'That should hold things until you can get a permanent repair done,' he said, walking back with her into the kitchen. 'At least the storm's beginning to move on…it's heading further up the coast, I imagine. We've had the worst of it here, I think.'

His mobile phone was on the table, flashing to show that another message had been received.

'Do you need to answer that text message?' she asked. 'It might be important.'

'Yes, you're right. Perhaps I should. I'm not on call right now, but given the circumstances…' He glanced at his phone and read the message on screen, then winced. 'It's the hospital—they texted earlier—there's been an influx of patients injured in the storm and they're putting out a general call for any medics available to go and help.'

'So you'll be going back there? Will it be safe for you to drive?' She was worried for him, but knew instinctively that he wouldn't be comfortable staying here with her when there were patients who needed him.

'I expect so—I don't really have a choice. I have to go and help out.' He frowned. 'I don't want to leave you here,' he said. 'If the storm doubles back for any reason that roof could be totally destroyed. I'd feel much happier if you were to come and stay up at the plantation house until things are sorted here.'

She shook her head. 'Thanks for the offer, but I can't go anywhere—what would I do about Emma?' She wasn't thinking clearly, was concerned for her sister, worried about leaving the cabin, and anxious because she knew she ought to go and help out in the emergency. 'I haven't been able to get in touch with her. She won't know what's happening. Anyway, I'm sure I'll be all right staying here now that the roof leaks have been sorted.'

'No, you won't,' he said firmly. 'That's only a temporary fix.' He reached for her, grasping her arms in a gentle but firm hold. 'You can leave a note for Emma to tell her where you are. Apart from the risk of the roof giving out, the power is still down. At least up at the plantation house we have a generator for when the electricity cuts out. Emma will be fine, I'm sure. The phones are probably temporarily out where she is—I expect you'll be able to talk to her soon enough.'

'I don't know...' Her brow furrowed. 'I need to see her...make sure she's all right. It isn't like her not to keep in touch. I need to go up to the village and try to find her.'

'But not right now—in the middle of a storm.' He tugged her close to him. 'Think about it, Rebecca... You can't stay here, and you won't be able to get in touch with your sister until things

calm down a bit. You have to come with me—
let me take care of you.'

She shook her head. 'I don't need you to tell
me what to do, Cade. I'll be perfectly all right
here now that the storm's moving on. I can look
after myself.'

'Sure, you can… But there's no way I'm going
to leave you here alone. These storms are fickle.
You don't know what might happen.' He looked
down at her, his eyes sparking with determination. 'You can't stay here. I won't let you.'

'Oh, really?' She raised her brows. 'I don't see
that you have a choice. It's *my* decision to make,
not yours.'

'Is it? Maybe I can persuade you otherwise…'

Before she had time to realise his intention he
swooped, claiming her mouth in a fierce, possessive kiss that caused the blood to course through
her body in an overwhelming tide of heat. Her
lips parted beneath the sensual onslaught and
she clung to him as her limbs responded by
trembling under the passionate intensity of his
embrace.

It was like nothing she'd ever experienced before. His kisses made her feverish with desire, the touch of his hands turned her flesh to fire as they shaped her curves, leaving her desperate for more. It was so unexpected—such a coaxing, tantalising raid on her defences. Her resistance crumbled. She wanted to stay here, locked in his arms, having him hold her, with his long, hard body pressuring hers and promising heaven on earth.

But these moments of bliss came to an abrupt halt as an almighty crash rocked the wall of the cabin. She froze, shocked into stillness by the noise and the sheer terror of wondering what might have happened.

'The storm—' she said. 'The wall—surely it's strong enough to stand up to the storm? Something must have happened outside—some damage—'

'It's probably a tree that's come down.' Reluctantly, he released her, then went to the kitchen door and looked out. 'I was right,' he said, closing the door abruptly. 'The wind must have weakened it and finally it collapsed. We need to get out of here, Rebecca. You know what I'm saying makes sense, don't you?'

She nodded. 'Yes, okay. I suppose so.' Even *she* couldn't argue if trees were crashing down around them. Who could tell if the cabin wall would give way at some point? There were trees surrounding the house.

'I'll get your cases and load them into the car.' He started towards the bedroom. 'Is there anything else you need to take with you?'

'No, I don't think so.'

'You'll need a jacket—the wind's dying down, but it's still raining out there.' He pulled his own jacket from the back of the chair and shrugged it on.

She nodded. She could hear the rain, still frantic, hitting the roof shingles and spattering against the door and the shutters. 'Okay. I'll get it. But maybe we should head for the hospital—I'm a medic…I could help.'

'I'd rather you didn't—for whatever reason, you've turned your back on medicine for a while.

Besides, you're not familiar with the terrain out here…the way things operate…and anyway I'd feel better if I knew you were safe up at the plantation house. It will be one less worry for me.'

She frowned. 'I'm sure I could make myself useful in some way.'

Perhaps the people up at the plantation would need help of some sort. If he didn't want her working alongside him, at least she could offer support where it was needed.

They hurried out to the car a minute or so later and he stacked her luggage in the boot, alongside his medical bag and equipment. She took a moment to take a quick glance around. Most of the garden had withstood the brunt of the storm, but a couple of trees had succumbed to the elements, which had left several branches twisted and torn. One of them had split along the length of its trunk and fallen against the cabin wall.

Cade set out along the road to the plantation. It was disturbing to see the destruction in some places along the way. Crops were ruined, plantains and banana trees had been brought down.

Fields were flooded where rivers had over-flowed, and landslides had caused devastation. In one part the road was blocked by an accumulation of detritus that Cade had to toss to one side so that they could continue their journey.

She slid out of the car and went to stand at his side. 'There's no need for both of us to get wet,' he said, but she helped him move the debris despite his protests.

They set off once again, driving ever higher into the hills, and soon came to a small settlement. A dozen or so houses were clustered in what in any other circumstances would have been a breathtakingly lovely part of the island, where several waterfalls cascaded into a blue lake.

'Look—over there…' Rebecca pointed to what looked like an abandoned car, slewed at an angle where a slip road veered off to the west and formed a narrow bridge over a stream. 'Something's wrong. We should stop and take a look.'

He nodded, edging his SUV on to the slip road and following it as far as he could do so safely. Further on the road's surface disappeared under a tangle of broken concrete and stone. The bridge had collapsed and water flowed all around, swamping the saloon car that had apparently been heading towards the village in the distance. As the bridge had collapsed the car must have been hurled into the water, and now it was tilted precariously on one side, lifted up at its front end by a grassy mound.

As they moved closer Rebecca pulled a swift intake of air into her lungs. 'There are people still in the car,' she said urgently. 'We have to help them.'

Cade brought the car to a standstill on a dry stretch of the road above the level of the water. He was already getting out of the SUV as she spoke, and grabbing his medical bag from the boot before heading towards the car. Rebecca followed, gasping as the cold water swirled around her denim-clad legs and slowed her progress.

She waded forward, peering into the stranded vehicle. There were signs of movement inside.

A youngish man—the driver—was slumped to one side, leaning towards the passenger seat, a trickle of blood running down his temple. Beside him a woman was apparently unconscious. The back of the car was under water.

Rebecca pulled at the doors but they were jammed solid. 'They must have locked automatically, somehow.'

'I'll get a wrench,' Cade said. 'We'll have to smash the side windows.'

He ran back to his vehicle and returned a moment later to swing the wrench at the glass. It gave way, shattering into a thousand pieces, and quickly Cade cleared a gap so that he could reach in and release the door catch.

The man began to come round. 'What's happening?' he said. Then, as his thoughts became more focussed, he added, 'The bridge—'

'You've been in an accident,' Cade told him. 'You've banged your head. Are you hurt anywhere else?'

'Just a headache,' the man answered. Then suddenly, 'My wife—Jane—' He looked around. 'I think she's bleeding.' He was dazed and shocked, not thinking clearly.

Cade helped the man out of the car and, seeing that he was going to take care of him, Rebecca slid into the driver's seat so that she could tend to the passenger. The woman's airway was clear, she was breathing fitfully and there was a faint, erratic pulse. After a while, she stirred, and Rebecca gave a swift sigh of relief.

'Jane,' she said urgently, 'are you in pain at all?'

'It…hurts…to breathe,' the woman said. 'My chest…hurts.'

Rebecca quickly checked her over. 'I think you've broken some of your ribs, Jane,' she said. 'Don't worry. We'll get you to hospital.'

'My baby…?' The woman frowned. 'Is my baby all right?'

'Your baby?' Rebecca echoed. 'Are you pregnant?'

'No…no…my *baby*…' She tried to twist around, gasping in pain at the effort, and with dawning horror Rebecca realised that she was looking at the back seat. It was completely sub-merged in water.

'Oh, no...'

She started to slide out of the driver's seat, but Cade was already on his way. The man must have told him about the infant because he looked shocked to the core, determination written in the clenched set of his jaw as he wrenched open the back door of the car.

'There's a child seat,' he said. 'I just need to feel for the release catch.'

It seemed like an age to Rebecca that he strug-gled to locate and press the buttons that would free the seat, but it must have been only sec-onds. He lifted the baby seat out of the water and she gasped as she saw the limp, lifeless form of the child fastened in there, her head lolling backwards, golden curls plastered wetly to her deathly white forehead.

'No, no...no... This can't be happening.' Re-becca was out of the car now, trying desper-ately to get to the baby, her legs hampered by the strong current of the water that eddied all around her.

'I have her,' Cade said briskly. 'I'll take care of her. See to the woman.'

It was like a cold slap across the face, bringing her to her senses.

'See to the woman. Get her out of the car. Get her and the man out of danger.'

She did as he said, moving like an automaton, but all the while her mind was on the child. She wanted to be with her, looking after her. The child was about a year old, with pale, chubby cheeks, and there was a bluish tinge to her rosebud mouth. Rebecca's heart squeezed in anguish. It wasn't fair. It wasn't right. Things like this should never happen.

She led the man and his wife to safety and sat them down on a grassy hillock set back from the water. The man was showing signs of concussion, the woman coping with the effects of the broken ribs that hampered her breathing. They were supposedly the lucky ones...if you could call losing a child anything remotely to do with luck.

She felt sick, her lungs heaving with the effort of holding back her emotions. 'I'll get something to cover you,' she said, aware that both the survivors might go into deep shock at any time. 'Stay there.'

'But my little girl—' The woman called out in desperation.

'We'll take care of her. I'll be back in a minute.'

Cade was working on the child. He'd taken her out of the car seat and laid her flat on her back on the ground near to his SUV. He was giving chest compressions. She heard the whispered rhythm of his voice as he accompanied his actions by counting the number of times he pressed down on the infant's chest with two fingers.

'Twenty-eight, twenty-nine, thirty...' Two breaths into the baby's mouth. Then he started the chest compressions again. 'One, two, three, four...'

Rebecca searched in the boot of his car and

opened up his medical bag. Her hands were shaking, but she managed to find two carefully folded foil blankets. She didn't dare think any more about what was going on with the child. It was heartbreaking to witness Cade's efforts.

'Twelve…thirteen…fourteen…'

He was doing everything he could for the baby. Was it too late? How long had she been underwater? She couldn't bear to dwell on it.

'I'll phone the hospital to tell them to expect us,' she told him, and he nodded, not stopping for a second, keeping up the compressions in perfect rhythmic timing.

'Twenty-nine…thirty.' Two breaths.

Hurrying back to the parents, she wrapped the heat-retaining blankets around them and gave them what comfort she could. They were desperate to be with their child, but both were dazed and injured and in no fit state to go anywhere without help just then.

Moving away so that they couldn't hear, she phoned the hospital and told the emergency team that they were bringing in an infant, suspected drowning, an adult with broken ribs, query internal injuries, and a man with concussion from a head injury.

She looked over to where Cade was working on the infant and heard a choking sound. Hurrying back to him, she saw that he was lying her down in the recovery position on her left side. She had vomited.

'Is she breathing?' she asked in a strained voice, hardly daring to believe it was possible.

'Yes,' he said simply. 'She suddenly choked and coughed up water from her lungs. Will you get the oxygen and an infant mask for me from the medical pack?'

'Of course.'

Going quickly to the back of his car, she searched the emergency response kit once more. A tear trickled down her cheek and she dashed it away.

'We don't know how long she was without oxygen, do we?' she asked, handing him the equipment he needed. There was the awful possibility that the little girl could have suffered brain damage… 'But the water was cold…'

'Yes, that will have helped.'

The cold water would have the effect of stimulating the diving reflex in a young child, slowing the heartrate and constricting the peripheral arteries, so that oxygenated blood was diverted to the heart and brain where it was most needed. There was a chance she would be all right.

She watched for a moment as he gave the baby oxygen through the small face mask. Then she said, 'I should go and talk to the parents. I'll start to get them into your car.'

He nodded. 'I'll feel happier if you sit in the back with the mother and the baby—the father can go in front with me.'

'Okay.'

He looked at her, studying her thoughtfully, a frown creasing his brow. 'Are you all right?'

The question startled her for a second or two. Of course she was distraught—seeing the baby in that condition had totally unnerved her. But she realised that she had subconsciously laid a hand over her abdomen. Perhaps it was meant to be a protective hand, laid over her womb—over that place which might never hold a child.

Sometimes she thought she felt pain where the adhesions left by her former illness had marred her fallopian tubes, but it might be a purely psychological reaction. It would be so much worse to give birth to a child, to nurture it and then to lose it in such a dreadful manner as these parents had almost experienced—might yet still experience.

'Yes, I'm okay. I'm just anxious to get this family to safety.' She looked at him, full of respect and awe for what he had achieved. The baby wasn't out of danger yet by a long way, but her lips had begun to pink up a little and her cheeks were less pale than before. 'You did a wonderful thing just now. I'm so overwhelmed by how you responded. You were so calm, so determined.'

'You would have done the same thing. As I recall you were ready to leave the adults to come and help the child… It was instinctive once you knew the parents weren't in immediate danger.'

She reached for another, smaller foil blanket from his pack. 'We should try to warm her—take off her wet clothes and wrap her in the blanket,' she said. 'She needs to be in the hospital.'

'Yes, we'll do that. And we'll be on our way in a minute or two. I just want to make sure she's stable before we set off. Her heartrate is a bit erratic at the moment, but it will probably settle once she's less chilled.'

They worked together to get everyone settled in his SUV. Reunited with her baby, the mother laid a gentle hand on the child, needing a connection of some sort despite the discomfort of her own injuries.

'Her name's Annie,' she said. 'She's my angel.'

Rebecca sat on the other side of the child, holding the oxygen mask in place and making sure that she was still breathing. The infant's pulse was slow—a protective reflex, no doubt—but once she was in the hospital the emergency team would do everything they could to resuscitate her. There was always the danger of pneumonia after a near drowning. The lungs had been flooded with water and there would be constant worry about the after-effects.

The journey seemed interminable, but in fact it only took around three quarters of an hour. Cade drove as swiftly as he dared, negotiating bends in the road and checking all the time for trees that might have come down along the way. Twice they had to get out and move fallen branches from the road.

Eventually, though, they arrived at the hospital and handed over their charges to the waiting team of doctors and nurses. Annie was whisked away to the resuscitation room and her parents were taken to Radiology for X-rays.

'I could take you home,' Cade said, 'but I expect you'll want to wait for news of how Annie's doing?'

'Yes, please… I'd rather wait. I don't think I could settle, otherwise.'

He nodded. 'Me, too. We'll go to my office.

They'll come and find us when they have some information.'

'Okay.' She went with him along the corridor, not fully aware of how she'd arrived there, just putting one foot in front of another. The last hour had been traumatic. The child's parents must be feeling as though they were caught up in a nightmare.

He showed her into his office—a light, comfortably furnished room with a polished wooden desk to one side and a couple of upholstered chairs for visitors. There was also a two-seater couch against one wall. He shut the door and she stared blankly around her, not really taking anything in.

'You probably want to go and help your colleagues with all their other patients,' she said quietly, trying to gather her thoughts. 'I'll just stay here for a while and get myself together, if that's all right?'

'I'll stay until I know you're okay,' Cade said. 'I wondered if it all might be too much for you.' He came over to her and wrapped his arms around her. 'You're too emotionally involved with your patients, aren't you? Is that why you gave up on your job?'

'I don't…I can't talk about it,' she said huskily. 'Please don't ask me. I can't even think straight right now. I just—I just need to know that little girl is going to be all right.'

'I know.' He held her tight, as though he would give her his strength and the will to go on. 'I feel the same way. I'm worried about her, but I'm concerned about *you*, too, Rebecca. I want to help you any way I can. You can trust me… I need you to know that.'

She didn't answer him. She closed her eyes and pressed her cheek against his shirt-front, wishing that things could be different… It would be such a relief to know that she could put her faith in someone—know that it would all come out all right in the end. But deep down she knew that wasn't going to happen.

Cade was a good man, but he couldn't turn her life around, and he had his own problems and aspirations to deal with.

CHAPTER FOUR

REBECCA WENT WITH Cade over to the couch, where he sat down beside her. He'd managed to find some fresh clothes for them to change into—clean scrubs, the outfits made up of the loose-fitting trousers and shirts that were used by the medical staff in the Emergency Unit—and now that she was at least dry she was beginning to feel a little better.

He laid an arm around her shoulders in a gesture that seemed entirely natural and right, and she was content for the moment to sit and talk to him and try to regain her emotional strength.

Her reaction to the events of the day had unnerved her. She had always thought of herself as decisive and independent, but over the course of the last few months she felt as though the stuffing had been knocked out of her. Somehow Cade must have picked up on that.

'How are you feeling now?' he asked. 'That was traumatic, wasn't it?'

She nodded. 'I'm okay. It was difficult for both of us. Are *you* all right? It must have been so much worse for you...trying to save the little girl...not knowing if she would breathe again.'

'I just did what had to be done. You don't really think about it, do you, when you're faced with something like that? Like you said about that man on the plane—you follow your instincts, go with the training.'

'Yes, I suppose so... But it was awesome, what you did. You kept going. You didn't give up for a second. I'm so proud of you.'

'I'm a doctor,' he said simply. 'That's the reason I took up medicine...to save lives and help where I can.' He looked at her, lifting a hand to gently ease back the fiery curls that fell across her temple. 'I was worried about you, Rebecca. You were upset and anxious for the baby, but there was more to it than that, wasn't there?

Something was troubling you deep down inside, at your very core—I wish you would talk to me about it, tell me what's wrong. Is it something to do with the reason you gave up your job back home? Did you lose a patient…a child in your care?'

She didn't answer him directly. It hurt too much to tell him the truth about her situation, and perhaps she was afraid it would change the way he felt about her.

'It happens sometimes…occasionally,' she said. 'You lose a patient despite everyone's best efforts. You do everything you can but there's nothing you can do if your best is not enough. There are times when medical science doesn't provide the answer.'

A knock at the door interrupted her and she tensed, brought back with a jolt to the reality of where they were. Cade eased himself away from her and instantly she felt the loss of his warm body and his gentle support. It was a wrench, losing the comfort of his embrace. She'd wanted to stay like that, wrapped up in his arms.

'Hi, Cade.' The consultant in charge of baby Annie's care came into the room. 'I only have a minute or two—things are hectic out there.'

'Hi, James.' Cade introduced Rebecca to his friend and colleague, who acknowledged her with a smile.

'I'm very pleased to meet you. Cade said you were the one who pointed out the car and saw that the family was in trouble.' James became serious. 'I came to let you know that we're doing everything we can to warm the baby. I've just been to talk to the parents, to try to reassure them, but it will be some time before we see any definite change in her condition.' He winced. 'She's lucky to be alive.'

Cade nodded, getting to his feet and going over to a worktop at the side of the room to switch on a coffee machine. 'We thought she'd already gone when we found her. It was a shock for both of us.' He set out mugs on the counter. 'Do you have time to grab a coffee?'

'Just a quick one, thanks. I can imagine how you must have felt. But, as I said, we're doing all we can. We're giving her warmed oxygen and an infusion of warmed intravenous fluids, so her core temperature should begin to rise gradually. We'll just have to hope there are no complications—and at the same time be prepared for them. There are often setbacks in these cases, unfortunately.'

Rebecca shuddered inwardly. She didn't want to dwell on that. All her hopes rested on the baby making a complete recovery.

They drank coffee and he updated them on the condition of the infant's parents. 'Mrs Tennyson has three fractured ribs, and her husband is suffering from concussion—as you suspected. They've both been given painkillers, and we'll keep them under observation for a while to make sure there are no other problems. Of course they're not going anywhere for some time— they're at Annie's bedside.'

'It sounds as though they're in good hands,' Rebecca commented, 'even though you must have a lot more patients than usual to look after. I noticed all the people milling about in the waiting room and in the corridors.' She'd seen men and women nursing injuries to arms and legs, and children with a number of bad cuts and grazes. 'It must be a difficult time for you.'

'You're right—it is. We've put out a call for more doctors—it's been difficult for some to get in, though, given the condition of the roads.'

'Well, *I'm* here,' Cade said. 'I can help.'

'Me, too.' Rebecca said, and saw the surprise on his colleague's face. 'I'm a doctor,' she explained, 'though my specialty's not emergency. If you can get me clearance, I'm happy to help out wherever I'm needed.'

She would rather do that than wait around, wondering what was happening with the baby.

'That's great news.' James's face lit up with enthusiasm. 'I can sort that out for you right away if you're sure you want to do that? We need as many medics as we can get.' Then he frowned. 'Do you have any training in obstetrics? We have a woman being brought in by ambulance—she went into labour several hours ago but only called for the ambulance when the contractions started to get more frequent. It's her first child. We're trying to get hold of an obstetrician to attend her as soon as she gets here, but they're swamped in Maternity.'

He looked at her hopefully.

'We really need someone to attend her as soon as possible. The paramedics are looking after her just now, but from what they've said when they radioed in it looks as though it might be a difficult birth.'

She felt the blood drain from her face, and her stomach lurched at the mention of obstetrics, but she nodded. 'I did a specialist course before going on to do my neonatal training. I'll go and see her, if you want.'

Cade sent her a narrow-eyed look and she braced herself. He must be wondering why she'd paled, but she hoped he wouldn't ask. When she'd volunteered she'd had in mind that she would be working with trauma patients—not mothers and babies—but she would do this despite her reservations. She didn't see that she had any choice. She couldn't stand by and do nothing when there was chaos and suffering all around her, could she?

'Bless you for that. She should be here any minute—I'll take you to the admissions ward now...and I'll get my secretary to sort out the necessary paperwork for you to sign.'

'Okay.' She pulled in a deep breath. 'Lead the way.'

They all walked along the corridor to the main area of the Emergency Unit, and James was pointing out the list of patients waiting to be seen when a nurse came up to them.

'We've had a call from the paramedics bringing Mrs Nelson in. Their vehicle has been hit by a tree—no one's hurt, but they're stuck out there. They're about a ten-minute drive away from the hospital. The birth's imminent, and it looks like a breech presentation.'

'Thanks, Greta.' James remained calm. 'Tell them I'll get someone out there to them.' He glanced at Rebecca. 'Are you up for it?'

'Yes—I guess so. But I'll need transport to get out to them.' She frowned. 'I don't know how easy it will be to get a taxi with conditions as they are.'

'I'll take you,' Cade said briskly, stepping forward. 'If it's a breech birth it may be better to have two of us present. I'll get directions—from the sound of things we should leave right away.'

'Okay.'

She went with him to the car park, keeping her head down against the wind that buffeted around them. The rain here was a steady downpour that quickly soaked through her jacket, but she ignored it, thinking ahead to the woman in the ambulance. A breech birth meant that the baby was not in the usual head-down position. Usually it would be best to deliver the infant by caesarean section—an operation that was the safest option for mother and baby. That was not going to be possible in these circumstances, when the woman's labour was far advanced.

'We'll be there in a few minutes.' Cade drove carefully to where the ambulance was stranded. 'Are you sure you're up for this?' he asked. 'I didn't want to say anything in front of James, but

I saw your reaction when he said it was a case for an obstetrician. I can take over if it's going to be a problem for you.'

'I wouldn't have offered if I wasn't up to it,' she said briskly. 'I'll be fine.'

'Okay. This is it, I think,' Cade said in a while.

They saw the ambulance on a straight stretch of a road that was lined with trees, and even in the darkness of late evening it was clear to see the devastation that had been caused to the side of the vehicle when a papaya tree had crashed down on to it. It was a miracle no one inside had been hurt, but no doubt a good deal of the equipment had been damaged.

The emergency services had been called out to deal with the accident, but so many similar incidents were taking up their resources that it would be some time before help arrived.

Rebecca slid out of the car and hurried to find her patient. The woman was being tended by the paramedics—a man and a woman—who stood to one side as Rebecca entered the ambulance.

'Hi, I'm Jimena,' the woman paramedic said.

She was tall, with curly black hair, and she looked strong and capable. 'We're *really* glad you could make it out here to us—aren't we, Kenzie?' She looked at her patient for confirmation.

Kenzie Nelson nodded. Beads of sweat had broken out on the young woman's brow and Rebecca guessed she was in pain from her contractions and under stress after the accident.

Jimena continued, 'We've been giving her gas and air, but it isn't really helping with the pain. Contractions are regular—every five minutes—she's six centimetres dilated, and her waters have broken.'

'It sounds as if things are well under way,' Rebecca said with an encouraging smile. She introduced herself and Cade, and then told Kenzie, 'I could give you an injection of pethidine into your thigh, if you like? That should help relieve the pain, but it might make you feel a bit sleepy.'

'Thanks, that would be good.'

'Okay.'

Rebecca prepared for the procedure, cleaning

her hands with antiseptic solution and pulling on surgical gloves, leaving Cade to gather together the rest of the equipment and the medication she would need. She examined the pregnant woman, checking her blood pressure and observing the contractions, as well as monitoring the foetal heartbeat. She made sure that Kenzie had understood that the baby would be delivered with either its bottom or its feet first. Apparently she didn't know the sex of the baby she was expecting.

'Everything seems fine,' she said, at last, hoping to reassure her patient. For herself, she had to prepare mentally for what lay ahead. Breech births could be tricky, and most doctors would prefer to deliver them in the safety of a hospital theatre.

She turned to the paramedics. 'Would you go on giving gas and air as she needs it? And perhaps one of you could see to it that we have suction apparatus to hand?'

'Will do.' They both nodded and the other paramedic, who was also the driver—Marcus—

said he would keep in touch with the hospital by radio.

'Thanks.' She glanced at Cade. 'Perhaps you could monitor her vital signs and keep an eye on the baby's condition?'

'Of course.' Cade was already preparing the woman, cleaning an area of skin on her thigh, ready for Rebecca to give the injection. 'It'll take a few minutes before you feel the effects of the pethidine,' he told Kenzie, 'but it's a good pain-reliever.'

It wasn't long before Kenzie's contractions became stronger, and soon they were coming at faster intervals. 'She's fully dilated,' Rebecca said. 'I can see the baby's bottom. I may need to do an episiotomy—a small cut,' she told Kenzie, 'to make it easier to deliver the baby. I'll anaesthetise the area first, so you won't feel it.'

She waited awhile, letting nature take its course, and then, as more of the infant's rear end came into view, presenting at a sideways angle, she carefully turned the baby so that its back was facing upwards—the safest position for delivery.

'I'm going to very gently insert a finger, so that I can bring down the baby's leg on the right side,' she told the woman. 'Are you okay?'

'I think so. I just want this to be over.'

'I can imagine… It shouldn't be too long now. You're doing really well.'

Rebecca concentrated on delivering the first leg, and then adjusted the baby's position once more to enable her to bring down the left leg more easily. It was a delicate manoeuvre, and she held her breath as she performed it, taking care not to cause any damage to either mother or baby.

'That's good,' Cade said, smiling his relief. 'Both legs are out safely,' he told the mother. 'Oh, and it's a boy!'

Kenzie gave a soft gasp of delight. 'A *boy*! That's what my husband was hoping for.'

'We'll let nature take its course for a while,' Rebecca said quietly.

Gradually more of the baby's body descended, until she could see an elbow peeping out. Two more careful manoeuvres and gentle turning motions helped bring down the infant's arms one by one. She let out a slow breath. Feeling her way, she placed her middle finger at the back of the baby's head and supported its body underneath with her forearm, placing two fingers either side of his nose. Then she slowly tilted the infant so that his head could be delivered fully.

Exposed to the air, he let out a protesting cry and Rebecca felt a lump forming in her throat. He was safe. He was perfect.

Quickly Cade suctioned the baby's nose and mouth and wrapped him in a blanket. Then he laid him in his mother's arms, smiling at her blissful expression. Kenzie was exhausted, but all the pain and difficulties of the last few hours receded in an instant as she held her newborn infant for the first time.

Rebecca watched Kenzie and her baby, a joyous picture of unity, and despite her happiness for them felt unbidden pain suddenly tug at her heart. Would she ever hold her own baby in her arms that way? How certain could the doctors be that it would never happen? Was it hopeless? They'd told her the scans weren't good—that her ovaries might be affected by scar tissue, too. It was a nightmare situation.

She'd debated the possibility of having surgery at some point in the future, but Drew hadn't been prepared to await the outcome. 'I'm sorry,' he'd said. 'I know it's not your fault but...I can't do this...'

He'd wanted perfection, and he had made her feel as if she was somehow defective. It made her wonder if all men would react in the same way...

She blinked, as though that would blot out the image before her, and made a determined effort to pull herself together. Perhaps, as Emma had said, events were still too raw in her mind. It had been several months since the break-up now, but she was still at a low ebb healthwise, and that had made things seem far worse.

Cade glanced at her. His pleasure at the birth was undimmed, but now his gaze was curious. He knew something was troubling her, but she ignored his unspoken question and brought her attention back to her patient.

'I can give you an injection to help the placenta come away,' she told Kenzie, and the new mother nodded. She was too absorbed in her baby to care very much either way, Rebecca guessed.

She gave her the injection, again in her thigh, and waited for a minute or two before clamping the cord. Delaying the clamping gave the baby a better initial blood supply from the placenta— one that was full of nutrients, especially iron.

Cade continued to monitor the baby's condition, but it looked as though the infant was fine. Once the placenta had come away, and the episiotomy cut had been stitched, Jimena stepped in to see to the mother, and Rebecca moved back to give her room.

The other paramedic, Marcus, had been talking on the radio for the last few minutes, keeping in touch with the hospital and the ambulance service, and now they all chuckled as he announced, 'Backup's arrived.'

He climbed down from the vehicle to go and greet the new ambulance crew. 'Sorry we took so long,' his colleague said. 'How are things going?'

'Mother and baby are both doing well.'

Rebecca cleaned up and then stepped down from the ambulance, conscious of Cade following close by. She gave a report on the mother's condition, and Cade did the same for the baby.

'He's a little cold,' he said, 'so he'll need to be warmed.'

'We'll make sure of it. Don't worry.'

'Thanks.'

They said their goodbyes and then walked quickly back to Cade's SUV.

'You did a great job back there,' he said as he set the car in motion. 'You were fantastic every step of the way.'

'Thanks. I'm just glad that things worked out all right.'

Darkness was all around them as they drove back along the country lanes towards the town, but it looked as though the rain was finally beginning to ease off. She settled back against the luxurious upholstery and closed her eyes briefly.

'Are you okay?' he asked. 'I thought something was bothering you, back there in the ambulance. Do you want to talk about it? I wish you would let me help you.'

'No. It's all right. I'm fine—really. It's just been a difficult day, that's all.'

It was the truth. The day had seemed endless already—full of worries, problems and complications—and they still had to go back to the hospital and wait for news of baby Annie.

'And I'm still worried about Emma.' She fished her phone out of her pocket and tried calling her sister once more. 'I keep trying to get in touch with her,' she told Cade.

He must have guessed she was prevaricating, not wanting to talk about her other worries, but he said nothing more about it, driving on and concentrating on watching the road while she dialled and waited. And waited.

'Is she still not answering?' he asked.

'No.' She frowned. 'It's not like her not to phone me. I'm sure something's wrong.'

'As I said, the phone network may be down— or she may be busy, or sleeping. It's getting late now, you know.'

'Yes, perhaps you're right. But if I don't hear from her soon I think I'll have to go and find her…to make sure she's okay.'

She settled back in her seat once more, trying to calm herself and get some rest before they arrived back at the hospital. After a while her phone burbled and she checked the caller information.

'It's William,' she said.

'Ah.' He sent her a fleeting sideways glance, his brows drawing together. 'He probably wants to meet up with you again.'

'Yes, maybe…' She answered the call and chatted with William for a while, asking him about his work day and about his father's illness. In turn, he asked about Emma.

'I still haven't been able to get in touch with

her,' she told him. 'I shan't feel happy until I know she's okay.'

'I know how you feel,' William said, with more emotion in his voice than she'd expected. 'I'm worried about her, too. But it's probably nothing—just a problem with the phone signal in the village.'

'You're probably right,' she said. It was strange William was so worried about Emma, given that they didn't really know each other that well. Emma had that effect on people, though. She was friendly and caring and everyone seemed to like her.

'I could finish work at the plantation early tomorrow afternoon,' he said. 'Take you out to cheer you up. Maybe we could go to the beach once the storm clears up.'

'Bless you—you're an angel,' she said, smiling. 'It sounds wonderful. I'd like that.'

'Me, too,' he murmured.

She cut the call a minute or so later. Cade was frowning.

'Sounds as though you and William will be getting together again?' he said, and she nodded.

'He's promised to take me to the beach,' she said.

'Oh, I see.' He said it as though that bothered him. 'You and he get on really well together, don't you?'

'Well, we're friends. We have a lot in common with one another.'

'Hmm…'

She sensed that he was battling with feelings of jealousy. The way he had kissed her during the storm had been so full of raw passion and command, and yet he clearly felt unsure about what it had meant. As did she. It had played on her mind—and her senses—ever since. And no matter how much she insisted that she and William were just friends, it was clear his worries persisted.

His frown had deepened, and to divert his train of thought she said, 'He says his father is now being given corticosteroid medication to reduce the inflammation around his heart, and they've given him a different kind of tablet to regulate his heart rhythm.'

'Let's hope that will help things improve.'

He was quiet the rest of the way to the hospital, and she wondered if he was thinking about his uncle. It *was* a worrying situation.

Things were no better in Accident and Emergency.

'Annie's showing signs of pulmonary oedema,' said James, when they met up with the consultant once more in the Emergency Unit. 'It can happen, I'm afraid—as I'm sure you know—even several hours after being rescued from near drowning. We think a patient is doing okay, and then they suffer a downturn.'

Pulmonary oedema meant that there was fluid in the lung tissue, causing the infant to have difficulty breathing. It was what Rebecca had been dreading.

'Presumably you're giving her a diuretic to try to remove the water?' she said.

'Of course… Along with medication to stabilise her heart rhythm and regulate her blood pressure.' He laid a hand lightly on her shoulder. 'Believe me, we're doing everything we can for her.'

'I know…I'm sorry…I'm not doubting you…' She hesitated. 'Perhaps I should go and see to some of the other patients on your list? I need to keep busy.'

'All right. If you're sure.' James nodded. 'If you don't mind, I need to get on—so I'll leave it to Cade to show you the ropes.' He left them, hurrying away to see to the list of people who were waiting.

Cade frowned, studying her closely. 'Don't you think you've had enough for one day? It's very late—I could take you home. I've already rung Harriet to ask her to get a guest room ready for you. She'll have some supper put by for us, too.'

She shook her head. 'I don't want to go anywhere until I know Annie's all right.'

'Okay…' he said doubtfully. 'But if it gets too much for you there's always the couch in my office. If you need anything at all, you must let me know.'

She glanced at him. 'I will—but you don't need to worry about me, you know. I'll be fine. You're the one who needs to take time out and get your head down for a few hours—you came to the cabin to see me after being on call. To be honest, I don't know how you're managing to keep going.'

He gave a crooked smile. 'Years of practice,' he said, 'along with supreme body fitness, of course… From my regular workouts, great energy levels, vitality, suppleness…' He was struggling to keep a straight face.

'Yeah, yeah…' She laughed and waved him away. There were patients waiting to be seen.

But she couldn't help but eye him surreptitiously as he walked away. He certainly was in good shape—lithe and supple, in top form. She was glad she wasn't his patient—he'd make any woman's heart race just by being in the same room with her.

They worked for a couple of hours into the night, seeing to patients who had been injured in the storm and coming across one another briefly as they compared notes or when he signed her treatment records.

'Shall we go and look in on Annie?' he suggested. 'Her parents are with her doctors at the moment, so there'll just be nurses with her.'

She nodded. 'Have you heard anything? Has James said any more about how she's doing?'

'He says she seems to be responding to the treatment.'

Encouraged, she went with him to the observation ward, where the baby lay in a cot, surrounded by monitors that showed her temperature, respiration rate, heartrate, blood pressure and blood oxygen level. She was sleeping, her pale cheeks showing small patches of pink colour.

'Her vital signs are coming up to something near normal,' she said, relief washing over her. 'She's going to survive—do we know if she's all right neurologically?'

Cade glanced through the baby's file. 'Apparently she recognises her parents, and she's responded to them. Things are looking good.'

'Thank heaven. That's so wonderful to know.' She gave a heartfelt sigh. 'It's been a nightmare. It feels like the whole day's been one long trauma.'

As a doctor, she was used to dealing with situations like these, but somehow over these last few months her emotional safety net had been shredded.

He must have read the self-doubt in her eyes, because he reached out to comfort her. 'Not much of a holiday for you, eh?' He laid an arm gently on her shoulder. 'Time to go home, I think. We could both do with some sleep. You'll feel a whole lot better in the morning.'

'I expect so.'

'I'm sure of it.'

He drove to the plantation, following the winding road up into the hills. The rain had slowed to a drizzle and the wind was dying down—the storm had lasted a relatively short time, by all accounts, but it had been bad enough to bring down bridges, flood roads and cause landslides that had created havoc.

'I'll phone my landlord first thing in the morning,' she said. 'I expect he'll want to organise repairs straight away.'

'It could take several days for him to fix things, you know. Tradesmen will be in demand all over the island.' He sent her a sideways glance, as though to gauge her reaction. 'It could mean you staying at the plantation house for around a week…possibly longer.'

'Oh, I see.' She frowned. 'I suppose I don't have many alternatives… So if you're all right with that…?'

'I'm more than happy for you to stay with me.'

The plantation house was lit by a lantern in the porch, and security lights sparked into life on the veranda as they came up the drive. Cade parked the car and showed her into the hallway, leaving her to look around while he went back to fetch her cases from the boot. It was a two-storey building, with a wide staircase leading from the central hallway to the upper floor.

'I'll show you to your guest room,' he said, hefting the cases as if they were lightweight. 'It's an en-suite room, so you'll have your own bathroom, and there's plenty of wardrobe space.'

He led the way to the room, setting her luggage down on the floor beside a double bed, and then showed her around.

'There are doors that open out on to the upper veranda,' he said. 'I think you'll love the view from here when you see it in the morning.'

'It's a lovely room,' she said, taking time to look around. There were voile drapes at the windows and beautiful silk covers on the bed to match the pale upholstery of the chairs and the dressing-table stool. A built-in dressing table and wardrobes took up the whole length of one wall.

'Harriet said she's left us some supper—cold cuts of meat and salad, with fruit for dessert. We could have it downstairs, in the kitchen, or I could bring a tray up here and you can help yourself whenever you're ready?'

'That's really thoughtful of you—and of Harriet. Thank you. I think I'd like a tray up here, if that's okay?'

'Of course.'

He came over to her and placed his hands lightly on her shoulders. If he was disappointed that she wasn't going to share the meal with him, he managed to hide it. There was just the faintest flicker of a shadow in his dark eyes as he looked at her. Perhaps he accepted that they were both tired after a difficult and draining day.

'You can have whatever you want. You did so well today...and I know it was hard for you. I'm not sure what went wrong for you in your job back home in England, but I sense you have a huge problem, working in obstetrics, don't you? I felt it in your reactions—but I know you don't want to talk about it...it's okay. I understand.'

He kissed her gently on the forehead, a kiss as light as thistledown, and she looked up at him in bemused wonder.

'What was that for?' she asked softly, and he gave a faint shrug.

'I just felt you needed it right now,' he said,

'and I want you to know that I'm here for you.' He straightened and reluctantly let her go. 'I'll leave you to get ready for bed and I'll bring supper up here for you. Don't worry if you're in the shower. I'll leave a tray on the table.'

'Thanks,' she murmured.

It seemed that she was in his debt yet again. He'd rescued her at the harbour on that first afternoon and he'd come to her aid today when the storm had damaged the shingles on the cabin roof. Now this.

She smiled tentatively as he turned to leave the room, but she was welling up with emotion inside. How had it happened that she had started to feel such tenderness and affection towards him? It was gratitude, surely, for everything he'd done for her…? But, no…it was more than that… much, much more.

It had been all too easy for her to grow attached to him, to want to have him close by. It was reassuring to know that he was only a heartbeat away.

She'd been so tempted to invite him to stay

with her…and he would have accepted in an instant, she knew. From the way he had kissed her earlier, and the tension in his body as he'd held her just now, she could tell he was also struggling to hold back.

But that would have led to all sorts of complications. It wouldn't do for her to fall for him, would it? That could bring about all kinds of heartache. It would be unbearable to love him and have it all go wrong when he learned that she was so terribly flawed.

CHAPTER FIVE

'HI, THERE.' CADE LOOKED across the room as Rebecca came into the kitchen the next morning. His eyes glinted approval, his gaze resting on her for a fraction longer than was necessary, taking in the curving lines of the pencil-slim skirt that hugged her hips and the sleeveless top with spaghetti straps that revealed a smooth expanse of golden skin.

The toaster pinged and he jumped slightly, distracted and disorientated for a second or two. Rebecca went over to him. It was somehow gratifying to know that she had such an effect on him.

He was obviously trying to multitask, toasting English muffins and whisking up what looked like a Hollandaise sauce at the same time. As she approached him she saw there were a couple of eggs gently poaching in a pan of hot water on the hob.

'Did you have a good night?' he asked.

'I did—thank you. I fell asleep as soon as my head touched the pillow. And you were right about the view from the French doors—it's fantastic.' She'd stepped on to the balcony first thing this morning and seen the rainforest laid out in front of her, sloping down the hillside, and in the distance the bay had been a vivid blue.

'I'm glad you took the time to look.' He smiled. 'I thought I would make eggs Benedict for breakfast…is that all right with you?'

'Oh, that sounds wonderful. I'm starving. It must be the fresh air that's giving me an appetite. You wouldn't know there had been a storm here, would you? Everything just looks as though it's been washed clean.'

He nodded. 'We get these storms from time to time, and after a downpour everything springs to life—plants and trees green up and flowers open.'

'It's beautiful.'

Sunlight streamed in through the tall windows and a warm breeze drifted in through the open glass doors. Out on the veranda she saw that a table had been laid with a white damask cloth, and there was a jug filled with fresh juice, along with two glasses.

Cade slid the hot buttered muffins on to plates that were warm from the oven and topped them with slices of smoked salmon. Then he added the lightly poached eggs, drizzled smooth Hollandaise sauce over the top and sprinkled chopped chives over that.

'Mmm…it looks and smells delicious.'

'Good…that's what I was aiming for. Let's eat outside, shall we?'

He led the way to the veranda, carrying the food on a tray that also contained a coffee pot and porcelain mugs. The aroma of freshly brewed coffee drifted on the air and Rebecca followed it as though mesmerised.

'This is heavenly,' she said as they sat down to eat. 'It must be the best way to start the day.'

This part of the veranda looked out over the

garden, a wonderful landscape of fruit trees—
lemon, tamarind and pineapple among them—
and there were palms that surrounded an
immaculate lawn area. Showy purple bougain-
villaea and scarlet kalanchoe brought colour to
the borders, along with sweet-scented pink and
yellow frangipani. The delicate fragrance drifted
over to them on soft air currents. In one corner
of the garden there was a lily pond bordered by
masses of bright pink sedum.

'I'm glad you like it. I was keen to get the plantation underway, but the house and garden were
my next priority. We're fortunate out here that
everything is so lush. Plants grow very quickly,
so it just takes a bit of landscaping and a gar-
dener who can keep on top of things to make it
all come together. I love sitting out here in the
mornings before work. It's tranquil, and it helps
to set me up for the day.'

'I can see why it would do that.' She savoured
the taste of the smooth sauce and runny egg
yolk on her tongue and sighed with satisfaction.

'This food is wonderful—I thought you said you couldn't cook?'

He shrugged, making a crooked smile. 'Let's say my repertoire is limited. I can manage a few egg recipes, pizza and maybe toss a pancake, so you wouldn't go hungry if you were relying on me. That's about my limit, though.'

'Perhaps you've never had much time to spend in the kitchen?'

'That's true—especially in the last couple of years, with my work on the plantation and the house.' He looked around. 'As I said, this place was pretty much run down and in need of some tender loving care when I took over. It's taken a while, but I think I finally have things on track.'

He poured coffee for her and she added cream and sugar. She said, 'From what I've seen so far it's a big house. It must have taken some doing to get it right. The kitchen is absolutely lovely. You have very good taste.'

He smiled. 'Thanks. I've always preferred light-coloured units, with display cabinets and plenty of glass shelving. And of course the central island unit is very useful.' He swallowed some coffee and then added, 'I'll show you around the rest of the house if you like?'

'That would be great, thank you—if you have the time. Do you have to go to work at the hospital today?'

'I'm on call this morning, and at some point I'll have to go in to deal with some paperwork. After that I have a couple of days' leave due to me—I'd planned to use it to finish off overseeing the building of my new fermentation sheds... though perhaps that's something William could get involved in.'

They finished breakfast a few minutes later and set off on their tour of the house.

The living room was long and wide, with three sets of French doors opening on to the veranda. They had been flung open to allow the warm air to circulate. The room was furnished along pale, uncluttered lines, with pale oak flooring and a corner sofa with matching armchairs. The coffee table was made of pale green-coloured glass, and that same green colour was reflected in the ferns placed at intervals around the room. Outside, beyond the veranda, there was more greenery, with graceful palm trees and yuccas and climbing philodendrons.

They went upstairs and he showed her several bedrooms, each with its own bathroom. They were all exquisitely furnished with stylish fabrics and restful colour schemes. Each room had doors opening out on to the wide balcony.

'This is breathtaking,' she said, looking around in wonder. 'The whole house is beautiful.' Her mouth curved as a thought struck her. 'I've no idea how you're going to fill all these rooms, though. Maybe you plan to have a lot of visitors?'

He smiled. 'I do have visitors, from time to time, but you're right, of course. It *is* a big house—but that's one of the things that drew me to buy this particular property.'

He leaned against one of the French doors in the main bedroom, looking out from the balcony over the forest and the curve of the bay in the distance.

'I like everything about it, and I'm hoping that perhaps one day I'll have a family of my own to fill it. It's not something I dwell on, or that I'm specifically planning, but it's there in the back of my mind—something to aim for. I didn't much like being an only child, but my parents' marriage broke up so there were never going to be any brothers or sisters. I want something different from that for my own future.'

She met his gaze as steadily as she could, with an equilibrium she didn't quite feel. 'Family's important to you,' she commented. Unaccountably, her heart was sinking. She should have known it was foolish to get to know and like him...to have deeper feelings for him. She was hurting already, and a heavy ache was starting up deep inside her. 'It's something that's been missing from your life.'

He nodded, moving away from the balcony and back into the bedroom. 'I suppose so. I haven't really analysed my feelings as such, but in the back of my mind I think I bought this house with the idea that it would be a happy family home one day.'

They went out into the hallway. She said slowly, 'Of course that would depend on you meeting the right woman. You *did* say you'd had some problems with that…'

He laughed. 'Well, yes. Perhaps I've been unlucky in the women I've dated so far.' He stopped on the landing, by the balustrade, his gaze meshing with hers. 'That could change, though. Who knows what life holds in store? After all, here I am with an incredibly beautiful girl—someone who's thoughtful, sweet-natured and caring—it's the stuff that dreams are made of.'

He moved closer, reaching for her, his hand resting on her waist, drawing her to him and folding her into his arms. He kissed her—a tender, coaxing, sweetly gentle kiss that stirred her senses and made her pulses rocket out of control. His hand stroked warmly along the curve of her spine, bringing her even closer to him so that her breasts were softly crushed against his chest and their thighs tangled.

The breath caught in her throat. For a moment—for a heartbeat in time—she almost gave in to her deepest desires and leaned into him. Then she came to her senses and reluctantly, with a feeling of angst rising inside her, put a hand on his chest to ward him off. She couldn't get involved with him. No matter how much she wanted to…she couldn't…

'It might not be,' she said softly.

He was teasing her, surely, and she batted away the notion of him wanting her before it had time to take hold. When he'd kissed her and held her back at the cabin, emotions had been running high. It didn't have to mean anything…did it?

'I'm not looking for a relationship, Cade,' she said flatly. 'I've been there, done that, and it all went very badly wrong for me. I don't think I want to dip my toe in that water again for quite some time.'

'Are you quite sure about that?' His eyes darkened and his hand gently stroked the rounded contour of her hip. 'Perhaps I could persuade you to change your mind?'

'Oh, I wouldn't bank on it,' she said, with a jauntiness she didn't feel. 'You know me—I'm here for a holiday…to have fun and take life as it comes. No strings attached, so to speak.'

She stepped back, moving away from him. It was too much of a temptation, being close to him this way, feeling the warm touch of his hand on her body. It made her want what she couldn't have, and she felt a sudden desperate need to escape. She turned around and started to go back down the stairs, conscious all the while that he was following her.

'And doing that will involve William, I suppose? *I* don't figure anywhere in the equation, do I?' His expression was taut, a muscle flicking briefly in his jaw. 'You want to be with *him*.'

It felt as though she was on a course of self-destruction, but she plunged on. 'Well, he did see me first—and he did offer to take me down to the beach this afternoon. I'm quite looking forward to that.'

It was cruel—a harsh way to treat him, perhaps—but wasn't this better than hurting him even more deeply in the long run? He wouldn't want her if he knew the truth about her, and she couldn't bring herself to tell him right now. Perhaps saying it out loud to a man she cared about would make it inevitable—the desperately dreadful aftermath of her illness. She didn't want to admit the finality of it even to herself.

He stared at her in an arrested fashion, thrown by her flippant reply. She might have slapped him, judging by the way he'd reacted. It seemed he was about to say something in response but his phone beeped and he hesitated, a soft, unspoken curse hovering on his lips.

'I should take this—it might be the hospital,' he said.

She nodded and he quickly checked the text message that had come up on screen.

She glanced at him after he'd put the phone back in his pocket. 'Was it the hospital?' she asked.

'No, but it's a call-out.'

Rebecca frowned. 'I'm sorry. You must go, of course.'

He braced himself, straightening his shoulders. 'I don't want to leave you stranded here,' he said. 'If you want to go out and about anywhere, I can arrange for Benjamin to drive you.'

'No.' She shook her head. 'There's no need for that. I'll have to sort out some form of transport while I'm on the island. I can't rely on you and William all the while. I'll see if I can rent a car.'

He was thoughtful for a second or two. 'Actually, it's just occurred to me,' he said. 'I have a four-wheel drive car you could use. It's a few years old, but it's been maintained well and it will get you around reliably. My uncle uses it sometimes, when he works on the plantation, but he's not up to driving at the moment. It's yours if you want it—until he's back on his feet again.'

'Oh...really? Thank you.'

She looked at him, a smile curving her lips. She didn't deserve his kindness. He was doing this for her despite their recent altercation, though she suspected part of his motive for making the offer was to make her less reliant on William... His cousin was more than willing to help her out, and Cade clearly wanted to nip that in the bud.

'That's settled, then,' he murmured. 'We have insurance to cover us for any driver, so there's no problem there.'

'You're being very good to me,' she said. 'And I do appreciate it, you know? It'll give me the chance to explore the island.' And maybe she could even go and look for Emma. That was her first priority.

He studied her, his brows drawing together. 'You're welcome. I should have thought of it before. The car's just sitting around in the garage at the moment…it'll be ideal for you to get around.' He seemed a touch hesitant as he added, 'It's probably best to avoid going up into the hills, though—especially right now. Road conditions will be tricky after the storm.'

He looked at her musingly for a moment or two longer, trying to gauge her thoughts, and she tried to put on an air of innocence. After all, he hadn't really been able to read her mind… had he?

'Have *you* driven up there?' she asked. 'Into the hills?'

He nodded. 'There are hairpin turns and in places there are sheer rock faces on either side of you, with vertical drops. It's not a drive for the faint-hearted.'

'Oh, I see.' She frowned, thinking about that.

She wasn't normally of a nervous disposition, but she balked at taking to roads where she wouldn't see a hedgerow or houses or at least something fairly solid on either side of her. But she hadn't heard from Emma for a few days now, and she was concerned about her. Something was wrong—she was sure of it… And, no matter that Cade had warned her against it, she would have to go in search of her sister sooner or later.

'It will be good to have a means of getting about, anyway. Thanks again.'

A frown cut into his brow but he simply said, 'We could go and take a look at the car right now, if you like?' He glanced at his watch. 'I have to go out to look at one of my workers who's been taken ill—the text message was from Harriet, to tell me about it. We could take the car for a spin over to his house if you want to get used to it.'

'Sounds like a great idea.'

She went with him to the garage—which turned out to be an old stable block at the back of the house. It had been renovated, and now accommodated a number of vehicles—including the new truck.

Cade stowed his medical bag in the boot of a smart silver-coloured vehicle and then handed her the keys. 'Okay, you're in charge. I'll give you directions on how to get there. Agwe lives in a village some six or seven miles away from here. It's a tourist area, where people go to fish in the river, and when he isn't working on the plantation he helps out with the catch. They run competitions and weigh the fish. Unfortunately his village was hit by the storm several hours before we were. There are flood waters all around.'

'Do you think we'll be able to get through to his home?'

'It should be possible. The bridge held up, and his house is on higher ground.'

'Okay.' She started the car, pleased when the engine fired into life straight away. 'What's wrong with him—do you know?'

He shook his head. 'The message was a bit vague. Flu-like symptoms, muscle pains, headache…'

'Do you treat *all* of your workers when they're ill?' She turned the car on to the road leading away from the plantation and set off towards the south of the island.

'I usually try to do what I can for them. Medical bills can be an unwanted expense—their insurance premiums might be affected by any claims they make—so if it's at all possible I'll help out. It's part of the package they get, working for me. So far things have worked out all right.'

The car handled well, she discovered, and once she was used to the gears and the instrumentation, things went smoothly. They reached Agwe's village only a few minutes later.

'Thank you so much for coming,' his wife said. She was a middle-aged woman, with springy black hair and dark hazel eyes. 'Come in…come in.' She ushered them into a small cottage. 'I'm really worried about him. I thought maybe he needed to go to the hospital—but he won't listen to me. He says he doesn't want to be a burden to anyone.'

'He's not a burden, Marisha,' Cade said. 'Has his condition worsened in the last few hours?'

She nodded. 'Yes, I think it has. He's feverish. He's not well at all.' She led the way to the bedroom. 'He was taken ill yesterday. We thought it was just a virus, and it would pass, but he seems to have gone downhill since then.'

At Marisha's invitation Rebecca went with Cade into Agwe's bedroom. The woman hovered in the doorway.

Her husband was lying in bed, beads of perspiration breaking out on his forehead. 'Hi, Agwe,' Cade said, going over to him. 'I'm sorry to hear you're not well.'

Agwe mumbled a response. 'My wife shouldn't have bothered you. I'll be fine.'

'You don't *look* fine,' Cade answered. 'I'd like to examine you to see if I can help, if that's all right?'

Agwe nodded wearily, clearly unwell, and Cade started by taking his temperature and running a stethoscope over his chest. He checked his pulse and blood pressure.

'You're running a fever, and your heartrate is very fast,' he said after a while. 'Added to that, your blood pressure is low, and you say you're having problems with your waterworks—it seems as though you've picked up an infection of some sort.'

He looked at a graze on the man's hand.

'It's just a thought, but have you been handling fish from the river recently?'

'Yeah…a few days ago. I caught my hand on a fishing hook.' Agwe frowned. 'Why?' He was becoming breathless and finding it difficult to speak. 'Is it important?'

'I'm trying to work out what we're dealing

with,' Cade answered. 'There are a number of possibilities...but there have been one or two cases of Weil's disease admitted to the hospital recently, and your symptoms are similar. It's a bacterial infection that can be caught in various ways—through contact with contaminated water or soil, for instance. That graze of yours would have been an ideal entry point. I really think the best place for you is the hospital, Agwe.'

Agwe's wife said worriedly, 'So you think he has this disease?'

Cade nodded. 'It's very possible.' He turned back to Agwe. 'We need to get you to hospital so that they can do some tests and put you on intravenous antibiotics. I'm going to give you tablets to take right now, to start the treatment straight away.'

Agwe looked as though he was about to protest, but his wife stopped him with a look. 'Dr Byfield says you need to be in hospital, so that's where you're going. No argument.'

Cade smiled at the interchange and glanced at Rebecca. 'Are you up for driving there? It'll be quicker than waiting for an ambulance. I'll ring ahead to tell them to expect us.'

She nodded. 'Yes, I can do that—if you can make him comfortable in the back of the car.'

She knew Cade was worried about the possibility of kidney failure. Weil's disease could be very dangerous, and treatment should be started as soon as possible if there was to be a successful outcome.

They set off a few minutes later and Rebecca covered the distance in short time, thankful that the main roads had been cleared of debris. It hadn't taken her long to get used to the car, and she really appreciated Cade's offer to let her borrow it.

Once they reached the hospital Cade handed his patient over to the emergency team. The man's wife stayed with her husband, going to sit by his bedside.

'We'll bring in the renal consultant,' the doctor in charge of the team told Cade. 'I think you're probably right about the diagnosis—we'll start him on intravenous therapy straight away. He

may need corticosteroids, too. Thanks for bringing him in.'

'I was glad to help.'

Cade left Agwe in capable hands and went
over to Rebecca, who was waiting to one side.

'I have to stay and sort out my paperwork,' he
told her. 'It'll take me some time, so you might
want to take the car and get back to your holiday. I can make my own arrangements for getting back home. I'm sure someone here will drop
me off later.'

'I don't mind waiting,' she said, but he shook
his head.

'You've already done more than enough to
help out. Besides, I think I ought to stay around
here for a while, to see how Agwe's doing and
talk to his wife. She's upset, and could probably
do with knowing a bit more about what's likely
to happen to him. He'll be in hospital for a few
weeks, I expect.' He ran a hand down her arm
in an unexpectedly tender gesture. 'This is your
holiday. Go and enjoy it.'

'Are you sure you don't want me to stay?'

She frowned, uncertain about leaving him. Then it struck her that clearly he was no longer concerned about her seeing William this afternoon, and perversely that troubled her. Had she been all too successful in pushing him away from her? Wasn't it for the best? Then why did she feel so dreadful? Her stomach clenched in despair.

'I'm positive,' he said. 'Perhaps I'll see you at the house for dinner later this evening?'

She nodded, not willing to answer him outright. Now that she had a car at her disposal she only really had one thing in mind—as soon as possible she would go in search of her sister. She didn't want to involve Cade in what she was planning, because this was her problem to resolve on her own. Perhaps she was worrying unnecessarily, but she wouldn't rest until she was certain all was well.

She drove back to the plantation, stopping off to buy a few supplies, but hurrying because William would be arriving to take her to the beach in a short time. She thought about calling to put him off, but she didn't want to disappoint him. He was anxious about his father, and maybe some time at the beach would be good for him.

'Hey, it's good to see you, Becky!'

William arrived just as she'd finished packing a holdall with the things she thought she might need for a trek up into the hills. The storm might have caused problems up there—she didn't know what to expect—so she'd included a change of clothes, fresh water, food supplies... She put as much as she could cram in her backpack, together with medication she'd bought from the local pharmacy. She wanted to be prepared in case Emma was ill, or had been cut off by the storm. She couldn't imagine what had happened up there in the village, but if she'd been able Emma would have been in touch by now, she was sure.

William glanced at the holdall she'd left in a corner of the kitchen. 'Are you planning on leaving us?' he asked. 'I thought you were staying on the plantation for a few days.'

'That's the general idea,' she said, smiling,

hoping to throw him off track. She hadn't expected him to notice the bag. 'That's just a few things I've scrambled together in case I decide to go exploring.' It wasn't exactly a lie, was it? Although she had filled a backpack, too… 'There's such a lot of the island I haven't seen—including your beach…'

He laughed, taking the hint. 'Come on, then. It's perfect out there just now. The tide's out, and there's a soft, warm breeze.'

'Sounds idyllic. I'll just put this holdall up in my room and then we'll be off.'

They spent a couple of hours by the sea, alternating between splashing in the calm waters and lying on the sand and soaking up the sun. William went over to one of the tilting palm trees that grew along the shoreline and shimmied up the trunk to get to the coconuts. He picked one and brought it over to her, cracking it open on a rock and handing it to her so that she could drink the juice.

'Mmm…wonderful…' she murmured. 'I'm having the greatest time.'

'Me, too.' He was quiet for a moment or two. 'I bet Emma would love it here. She said how much she likes to spend time on the beaches around here. Have you any idea how long she was planning on staying up at the village?'

She shook her head. 'None at all. She didn't say.'

'I suppose her colleagues would have let you know if anything was wrong?'

'Yes, I'd have thought so.'

Only she hadn't been able to contact any of them. It was disturbing. There *was* the possibility that a phone signal wasn't available up there, but she couldn't help wondering if her sister had been taken ill or been involved in an accident of some sort.

William dropped her off at the plantation house and apologised for having to leave her so soon. 'Cade asked me to check on the new fermentation buildings,' he said, 'to make sure the workmen are doing everything according to the plans—and then I need to go with my mother to visit my father in hospital. He's on this new medication and we're hoping it's going to help him get better.'

'Good luck,' she told him. 'I hope things start picking up for him soon.'

After he'd gone she made a swift check to see if there was anything else she needed to take with her on her journey up into the hills. She quickly changed into jeans and a T-shirt and then downloaded a map from the Internet and printed it out. She hurried—she was anxious to get away before Cade returned from the hospital.

At last, she was ready. There were still about three hours left before sunset—surely it wouldn't take her more than an hour to make the drive up to the village? There would still be plenty of daylight to make the journey there *and* back, if need be.

She set off, driving carefully along a road that turned out to be exactly as Cade had predicted. It became progressively steeper as time went by, and there were potholes left by the recent storm, so she bumped and clattered and worried about the car's suspension. It was an all-terrain vehicle, though, so that shouldn't be a problem.

The landscape she passed through was awe-inspiring. She caught glimpses of mango and avocado trees being grown on small farms, and as she climbed higher into the hills saw slopes that were thickly forested with tall chataignier and spiky breadfruit trees. Vines grew everywhere, winding around tree trunks and climbing upwards towards the sunlight. As Cade had said, the tropical vegetation on the island was lush, thriving in the warm, humid atmosphere.

She drove on, and the road became more narrow and winding, with deep chasms falling away to one side. She slowed the car, alarmed by the increasingly craggy landscape and the towering cliffs that had been battered by the recent storm. As she went further, she saw there were landslips, where soil and rubble and other debris had accumulated in falls down the rock face. It looked precarious—as though it might tumble on to the road at any moment.

Rounding a tight bend, she held her breath

as she negotiated the difficult turn—and then gasped as she saw what lay up ahead. A large portion of the cliff had been undermined by rainwater and the softer sedimentary rock had sheered away from the volcanic grey basalt beneath. It had fallen across the road in a mass of boulders, tree roots, branches and rotting leaves.

She stopped the car and sat for a moment, debating what she should do. There was no way she could risk taking the car beyond this point, but she'd come too far to go back—she would have to go the rest of the way on foot.

She parked the car in as safe a place as she could find, as far off the road as possible, just in case anyone else might be as reckless as she and try to venture up further into what was virtually a small mountain. They would need room to turn around. Perhaps this was why Emma hadn't come home. The road was blocked.

Rebecca pulled on her backpack, took her holdall from the boot of the car and set off along the road. Even up here it was hot, and without the benefit of the car's air-conditioning she was wiping beads of perspiration from her face within half an hour. She sat down to rest on a flat outcrop of rock at the side of the road and gazed around her. She caught the green flash of a parrot's wings as it flew among the branches of the mountain cabbage palms. If only she could fly...

How much further was it to the village? According to the map it was only some twenty miles from the plantation, and she must have covered a good deal of the journey by now, surely? Perhaps she'd miscalculated somewhere... The sun was already getting low in the sky and she'd still not come across the small settlement of houses she was expecting to see.

Perhaps she ought to call someone and report that the road was blocked? She checked her phone, but there was no signal. She'd not really expected it to work up here, but it was a bit daunting to find that she was totally isolated, with darkness coming on. Had she been completely foolhardy to start out on this expedition?

She stood up and started on the road uphill once more. Cade would certainly have something to say about her actions when she finally returned to the plantation house. Her thoughts lingered on him. She felt strangely empty inside, with a feeling of unaccustomed loneliness washing through her. She missed him and wanted to be with him.

A soft sigh escaped her. He would have left the hospital some time ago. Was he wondering why she wasn't around to have dinner with him? Guilt ran through her. He'd been nothing but good to her and she'd pushed him away.

Lost in thought, she trundled on—until, bizarrely, from out of nowhere she heard someone calling to her.

'Hey, Rebecca! Wait…wait up…' The words cracked across the air like a whiplash.

She froze in her tracks, hearing that familiar deep voice coming out of the wilderness. It couldn't be Cade—could it? Was she hallucinating? Had she conjured him up out of pure wishful thinking?

Slowly, as though in a trance, she turned around and looked back at the road. Giant tree ferns covered the hillside, verdant among a stand of tall Caribbean pine. Then her glance settled on a lone figure and her heart leapt in her chest.

She shook her head briefly. This wasn't real. She was imagining he was there, surely? But, no, he was standing in the road, tall and broad-shouldered, his hefty medical pack slung over his back.

'Rebecca...thank heaven I've found you.' Cade walked briskly up to her, studying her from under dark brows. Putting his medical kit down on the ground beside him, he reached for her, his hands circling her bare arms. 'Are you okay? You don't look quite right.'

'It...it must be the shock of seeing you,' she answered huskily. 'I thought I was alone out here. How did you know where to find me?'

He gave a short, harsh laugh. 'It wasn't too difficult. I had the feeling you'd come after Emma. I guessed she'd been on your mind ever since she came up here. So when I got back to the house and you weren't there I rang William. He said you weren't still with him, but he told me you'd packed a holdall and taken it up to your room, so I went to check. It wasn't there, and it was fairly easy to guess the rest.' His mouth tightened. 'You've no idea how worried I've been.'

'There was no need for you to worry,' she protested. 'And you didn't need to follow me out here. This is my problem—not yours. I didn't want to involve anyone else.'

His eyes glittered, skating over her. 'Can't you imagine how concerned I was when I realised you'd taken it into your head to come up here?' He shook his head, tugging her close to him. 'How could I let you do this on your own? You've no idea what you might come up against. I've been so worried about you. This is a dangerous road and you're not used to the car.' His voice was edgy and tinged with impatience.

She looked into his smoke-dark eyes, trying to gauge the depth of his emotions. She was feeling overwhelmed. He'd actually come after her— had cared enough to make sure that she was safe—but he seemed to be rigid with tension.

'You're angry with me?'

'Angry? No. Not angry. Frustrated…concerned… It's getting late, and there's no way we can go back down that road in the dark. There could be another landslide at any moment and we need to be on the lookout for it.' He wrapped his arms around her. 'Rebecca, I was so afraid something might have happened to you…that you might be hurt…'

'But I'm fine—'

'You're *not* fine.' His tone was clipped. 'You're a pain in the neck, going off like that without a word. Anything could have happened.' He drew her up against him, holding her tightly, his whole body pressuring hers. 'I wish I didn't feel this way about you—but I can't help myself—'

He bent his head to hers and kissed her on the mouth, crushing her lips with intense passion—as though he couldn't get enough of her, as though he would rid himself of the demons that were driving him.

Her soft curves meshed with the hardness of his chest and her legs collided with the taut, powerful muscles of his thighs. A wave of heat ran through her from head to toe. She ought to be putting up some kind of a protest, she knew, even as she kissed him in return and lifted her arms to let her fingers caress the silky hair at his nape.

She was so glad that he was here, that he'd bothered to come after her. She'd been fully prepared to do this on her own, but now that he was with her she felt as though she could move mountains. He filled her with strength. Together, they could do anything…

Her body melted into his in an involuntary movement of longing, of deep, instinctive yearning. A soft moan rumbled in her throat. She wanted to run her hands all over him—over his arms, his chest—wanted to tell him how much she needed him, how glad she was that he was here with her.

His lips left a trail of kisses over her mouth, her cheek, her throat, and his hands made sweeping forays over her curves.

'I need you,' he said, the words hot against her cheek, and she felt her body tremble in response.

A soft, shuddery sigh escaped her. What was she doing? What was she thinking? How could she go down that road again? Falling for a man who would turn his back on her as soon as he learned the truth about her?

'I can't,' she whispered. 'I should never have let this happen.'

The breath caught in his throat and he stared down at her, his gaze hot with desire. 'Don't do this to me,' he said, his voice roughened. 'You kiss me as though you want me every bit as much as I want you, and then you change your mind and call a halt. You can't behave that way. You're driving me crazy.'

'I'm sorry.' She stared up at him, tears in her eyes. 'I'm *sorry*.'

He gave a ragged sigh and appeared to be making an effort to pull himself together. Slowly he put her away from him, holding her at arm's length.

'Okay,' he said. 'Explain it to me. You want to have fun. No strings attached. I can do that. I'm willing to give it a try. What's the problem?'

'It won't work,' she said, her chest heaving. 'Not with you and me. Not like that. It just won't work.'

He stared at her, trying to fathom what was going on in her head. 'Sooner or later,' he said, 'you're going to have to talk to me and tell me what's going on with you. Right now, I don't understand what makes you tick. But I *will* find out, Rebecca. That's a promise.'

CHAPTER SIX

'WE NEED TO find the village before nightfall.' Cade's tone was clipped, decisive.

'Yes. I'm not sure exactly how far it is.'

Rebecca sent him a swift glance as she picked up her holdall. Just a few moments ago he'd been holding her in his arms but now he was remote from her, as though he was steeling himself to keep a distance between them—at least physically.

He looked at the setting sun and lifted up his medical pack—it was a very large immediate-response kit, designed to provide every available means of helping patients in the dangerous time before they could reach a hospital.

'It looks as though you came prepared for trouble,' she said.

He nodded. 'I thought it was best to be on the safe side.'

She frowned as they set off once more along the road. 'But I thought you believed I was worrying unnecessarily?'

'No, that's not true. I didn't say that. I didn't want to upset you by agreeing that your sister might be having problems. There was no point in making you any more anxious than you already were.'

'But if I'd known you *agreed* she might be in difficulty I might have been persuaded to come up here earlier.' She sucked in a breath, upset by the waste of time. He knew this country and its idiosyncrasies far better than she did.

'You could hardly have come up here while the storm was raging. We couldn't even have got rescue helicopters in the air to check things out. Besides, as I recall we had our hands full—with a baby rescue and a breech delivery.'

'I suppose so,' she acknowledged, giving it some thought. His logic was unassailable.

They trudged up the hill, rounding a bend in

the road. A tarmacked path led off to the east, and they turned in that direction.

'It can't be far now,' she said, cheering up a bit. 'That's the landmark I was searching for. I knew there was a place where a side road turned towards the village.'

In the distance the land rose still higher, the slopes covered with luxuriant rainforest, broken only by the cascade of waterfalls that cut into the rock face and pooled far below into a wide lake. Just here a river tumbled down the hillside in a torrent fed by the recent rains. As Rebecca and Cade went further along the path it soon became clear that there had been a lot of flood damage up there.

'The path's been broken up by the water and the boulders that have been washed down,' Cade remarked. 'It'll be impossible to get supply trucks through here.'

Ahead of them they could see the outline of some painted wooden houses set out in a clearing.

The ground was now soft and muddy underfoot, and Rebecca stopped for a moment to pull a pair of boots from her backpack. She was wearing jeans and a T-shirt, and now she put on a light jacket. A light breeze had sprung up and she was beginning to feel apprehensive, not knowing what they might find when they reached the settlement.

'At least we should soon have some answers,' Cade said, glancing at her as they set off once more. 'It looks as though this place has been cut off by flood water—it's beginning to recede now, but from the state of the houses it must have been pretty bad while it lasted.'

He was right. It appeared most of the houses had been submerged up to a foot from the ground. There were dirty marks left on the houses' framework, from where the water had risen and then gradually started to ebb away.

'I expected to see more movement,' Rebecca commented. 'People going about the business of clearing up. Everything's so quiet…it's like a ghost town.'

'It's odd, definitely,' he agreed. 'Perhaps the

families moved out of the lower-lying houses into those on higher ground—out of the path of the water. There's some kind of communal building and a few dwellings over there that should have missed the worst of the damage.'

They headed towards the communal building—a large wooden structure. The entrance door swung open when Cade pushed it, and soon they were standing inside a long, wide room.

'This must be the school,' Rebecca murmured.

Desks had been pushed to one side to make space, and chairs were stacked neatly against the wall. Instead of being used as a place of learning, the hall had been turned into a hospital, with half a dozen beds arranged in a row, facing the windows. Three children lay in bed, covered by mosquito nets, whilst adults sat quietly next to them, reading or talking to one another in low voices. They looked up as the newcomers walked in, surveying them with tired interest. Two further beds contained adults who were sleeping.

Rebecca and Cade introduced themselves to

the people in the room. 'We're here to help—
any way we can,' Cade said.

A door at the end of the room opened, and
Rebecca drew in a sharp breath when she saw
Emma walk in. She was pushing a medicine
trolley, obviously trying to go about her work as
usual, but Rebecca was shocked by the change in
her sister. The vital, energetic and bright young
woman who'd been laughing and joking at Selwyn's Bar had disappeared completely, and
in her place was someone who looked ill and
drawn. She was very pale and looked intensely
weary, walking stiffly as though she was in pain.

Emma glanced across the room and saw the
visitors. Relief seemed to wash over her. 'Oh,
Becky,' she said in a choked voice. 'I *knew* you
would come. I knew if anyone could get through
it would be you.'

Rebecca went over to her sister and hugged
her. 'What are you doing up and about? You
don't look well,' she said. 'Why aren't the other
nurses looking after you?'

Emma shook her head. 'There's no one else

here—only the people you see in this room. When the floods came we had to evacuate as many people as we could to the next village.' She paused to get her breath. 'I said I would stay behind and take care of the patients. They were going to come back for me—but I think the villages must have been cut off from one another. They never came.'

She reached for a chair and sat down, suddenly losing strength.

'How long have you been feeling ill, Emma?' Cade asked.

'A few hours. It came on quickly. I'm tired, I suppose. I've been working through the night, looking after the patients.'

He frowned. 'From the state you're in, I think it's a lot more than tiredness. Do you have the same symptoms as the others?'

'No.' She tried to shake her head and cried out, wincing as pain shot through her. She held her hand to her neck and rubbed gently. 'The children have spotted tick fever. They're beginning to recover—I've been giving them antibiotics. They're due for another dose now… the adults, too.'

She started to get up to go to them but Cade gently pushed her back down.

'We'll see to all that. You need to rest. We have to find out what's wrong with you.'

'But it's time for their meal.' Emma's brow creased with anxiety. 'I've got to find something for them, but there's not much left—we're just about out of food.'

She drew in a shaky breath and shivered a little, wrapping her arms around herself for warmth.

'I've scrambled together what I could find, but the storehouse was flooded and everything was ruined. I don't know what we're going to do. The power's out, and the water pipe gave way on the first day—since then we've been managing with bottled water.'

She sank back in exhaustion.

'I've a couple of canisters of water and some food supplies in my holdall,' Rebecca told her. 'It's only protein bars and chocolate, and some nuts, but it's all high-energy stuff. It should keep everyone going for a while, at least.'

'And more help should be on its way before too long,' Cade put in.

Rebecca sent him a quizzical look. 'How can that be?'

'I have a friend who works with the air rescue service,' he explained. 'I called him from the hospital this afternoon and he said he would take the first opportunity to fly over the area and see if anyone was stranded. He said they were busy with other rescues, so he might not be able to do anything today, but he'll try tomorrow. We need to get something up on to a roof to show him there's a problem—something he'll be able to see in the daylight.'

Her eyes widened. 'So you've been thinking all along that there might be an emergency situation? You were never going to leave things to chance?'

'That's right.'

She frowned. 'You didn't tell me.'

'I wasn't sure I'd be able to reach him, or if

he'd be able to help. I would have told you if you'd been at the house when I came home.'

'I'm so glad you managed to get in touch with him.' She smiled at Cade and then said quietly, 'What should we put up on the roof?'

He thought for a moment, and then asked Emma, 'Are there any paint supplies around here? All the houses are painted, so I'm assuming there might be.'

'Yes. In the store room.'

'Good. I'll paint a large SOS on the roof.' He shot Rebecca a quick glance. 'Can I have a word with you? We need to sort out how we're going to organise things.'

She nodded, then turned to Emma. 'Stay here and rest. I'll come back and check you over in a minute—see if we can make you more comfortable. We'll see to everything so you don't need to worry… I'm assuming there are treatment charts for all the patients?'

'Yes, of course.'

Natural light was still coming in through the

windows, but Emma closed her eyes as though it was too bright for her.

'My head really hurts,' she said. 'I'm so glad you're here, Becky.'

Rebecca laid a hand on her shoulder. 'So am I. Get some rest. I'll be back before you know it.'

She went with Cade to stand a short distance away.

'I'm afraid your sister is very ill,' he said in a low voice. 'Whatever it is that's wrong with her, she needs treatment right away.'

She nodded. 'I know. I'm really worried about her—*and* about the other patients. We need to get things sorted quickly.'

'Okay. I'll do a medicine round and then see what food we have—if we hear a helicopter I'll go outside and wave my arms or something.'

'Thanks, Cade.'

She laid a hand on his arm in an affectionate gesture, but he stiffened at her touch and she gazed at him, disturbed by his reaction. She'd really hurt him in her rejection of him earlier.

He seemed to brace himself, and she took her hand away from him.

Taking a quick breath to steady herself, she said, 'Thanks for telling your friend about this. When I came out here I didn't know if I should be worried or not—whether I'd be able to handle things by myself. I'm so glad you decided to come after me.'

'I would never have left you to do this on your own. I'd already made up my mind to find out what was going on up here.' He frowned, studying her briefly, taking in her uncertain expression. 'Any time you have a problem I'll help you any way I can. I'll *always* help you—with anything.'

'Thank you,' she said softly.

She wished that could be true. How would he respond if she confided in him? If she told him that her illness had left her damaged, that she couldn't let herself fall in love with him? He wanted children, and that was something she couldn't promise him. She couldn't allow him to get involved with her, because in the end he would discover her deepest imperfection and then he would turn away from her—just as Drew had done.

She didn't think she could bear that. And nor could she cope with having an affair with him—a temporary fling—because already she cared too much for him. It would hurt too badly when it came to an end. Was it already too late? Had she already fallen in love with him? Why did this hurt so much?

'All right,' he said, straightening, ready to move on. 'Let's get on with this. Go to your sister—take my medical kit with you.'

'Thanks, I will.'

Rebecca hurried back to Emma. 'Where have you been sleeping?' she asked. 'I think we should get you to bed.'

'In the back room.' Emma started to get up, swaying a little and leaning on Rebecca for support. 'Oh…I feel really sick. I've been vomiting a lot. I can't seem to keep anything down.'

'I'll help you. Don't worry about it.' She waited with Emma while she was being sick in the bathroom, and then helped her into bed. 'I'll do a quick examination,' she told her.

Emma's hands and feet were cold, she discovered, but it was fairly clear she was running a fever. Things weren't looking good. Rebecca already had a horrible suspicion about what they were dealing with, but she put on a calm, reassuring front as she checked her sister over.

A few minutes later she packed away Cade's stethoscope and blood pressure machine and spoke gently, attempting to explain what she thought was wrong with her.

'Your blood pressure's low and your breathing and heartrate are quite fast,' she said. 'I'm pretty sure you have an infection—a bacterial infection—so I want to get you started on an intravenous antibiotic right away. I'm going to give you dexamethasone at the same time, to prevent any inflammation.'

Emma lay back against her pillows. 'You don't need to wrap it up in cotton wool for me, Becky,' she said, her breath coming in short bursts. 'I'm a nurse. I'm pretty sure I know what's wrong with me… It's meningitis, isn't it?'

Rebecca sighed softly and nodded. 'I think so. We won't know for certain until we get you to hospital and they do some tests, but we can't afford to take any chances. Luckily Cade has the medication we need in his kit, so we can start you on the treatment right away. All you need to do is try to get some sleep. I'll give you something for the headache.'

'Thanks, Becky.' Emma closed her eyes. 'It's so good to have you here…'

Rebecca stayed with her until she was sure she'd done everything she could, and then went in search of Cade.

She found him playing a card game—Snap— with one of the children, a boy of around five years old, who was sitting up in bed, recovering from his illness. They were laughing, because the boy was winning and Cade was pretending to be put out by it.

'We'll play again later,' he told the boy, and

stood up, leaving the child's mother to collect the cards and find a storybook to entertain him.

'Okay. I'll win again,' the boy said with a wide smile.

Cade chuckled and came over to Rebecca. His mood immediately became serious. 'How is she?' he asked.

'She's sleeping right now. I've put her on an IV drip and I'm giving her oxygen, but we need to get her to hospital as soon as possible.'

'Meningitis?' he guessed, and she nodded.

'I think so.'

The danger lay in the swelling of the protective membranes around the brain. This was causing Emma's bad headache, and if it became worse she might start having seizures. Then there was the awful worry about blood poisoning. That could cause all kinds of problems. Rebecca didn't even want to think about that.

'How are the other patients?' she asked.

'They're generally not too bad. It's a farming community, so the youngsters were exposed to tick bites from the goats their parents herd.

They're being given doxycycline to combat the infection. There are two five-year-old boys who are well on the way to recovery. The little girl is three years old—there's still some swelling on her leg, where she was bitten by a tick, and she's a bit fretful, having nightmares—they're part of the way the illness presents.'

'Really? I've never come across this kind of tick fever before.'

'Well, along with a high temperature and a rash, sufferers get bad headaches and muscle pain. The rash doesn't itch—which is a blessing, I suppose.' He looked over to the beds where the adults slept. 'Those two are suffering from chest infections. They're on oxygen and antibiotic therapy, as well.'

'It sounds as though everything's under control—what about the food situation? Did you manage to put a meal together?'

He pulled a face. 'After a fashion. I'll show you the facilities.' He walked with her towards a small kitchen at the back of the building and pushed open the door. 'There's no electricity, so

I've had to make do with very little. I thought we'd better save the protein bars for tomorrow.'

She nodded, glancing around. The room was utilitarian, with a deep sink, a cooker and a fridge—neither of which were working—and a counter for food preparation.

'Let's hope your friend gets here with a rescue team before too long. Heaven knows what we'll do if we have to stay here for any length of time.' She gave a shuddery breath, thinking of Emma.

He laid an arm around her shoulders. 'I'm sure we'll find a way to cope, whatever the situation. You had the foresight to bring provisions— I brought a medical kit. We make a good team, you and I, don't you think?'

'Yes, we do.' She pulled herself together. With him by her side she could move mountains. 'Do you want me to help you with painting the SOS? Maybe we need to do more than one?'

'No, I'll do it in a few minutes—before it gets dark. But first I should get you something to eat. I bet you haven't had anything since breakfast, have you?'

'Um…no, actually…' She hadn't even thought about eating until now. Maybe she'd been too stressed. 'I'm not really hungry—and anyway I need to stay with Emma.' Anxiety rose up inside her once again. 'I should get back to her.'

'That's okay. You can do that. I'll bring some food to you in there…see if I can tempt you with cold leftover rice and tinned peas.'

'Oh—stop…such a gourmet meal—how can I resist?' She gave a broken laugh in spite of her anxieties and he smiled.

'That's better—we'll get through this together…you'll see.' He looked into her eyes. They were damp with unshed tears and he said softly, 'I think you need a hug…would that be all right?'

She nodded wordlessly and he folded her against him, kissing her lightly on her forehead. 'We're doing everything we can for her—for all of them,' he said. 'You're doing fine—you're a great doctor and a good person to have around in a crisis.' He stroked her back, his hands gliding over her in a tender gesture. 'I can't think what your ex was thinking of, letting you slip away from him. Whatever happened between you must have destroyed your faith in men.'

'It wasn't Drew's fault—not really,' she said huskily. 'Things just didn't work out for us. He's a decent man, but things went wrong. I was ill—appendicitis—and there were complications. I ended up in intensive care for a while.' She sighed. 'He didn't handle my illness very well. I think I realised then that he wasn't the right man for me, but perhaps there were signs before that…we were opposites in quite a few ways. He could be quick-tempered and impatient, whereas I tend to be a bit more laid-back. With hindsight, I think we would have gone our separate ways before too long anyway.'

'I'm sorry. It sounds as though you cared for him very much and that finishing with him has had a bad effect on you. But it would be a pity if you're going to let it put you off all relationships.'

'Maybe.' She straightened. Talking about Drew was bringing back memories of things she would far sooner forget. 'I think I should go to Emma.'

'Yes. All right.' He let her go, easing his long body away from her. 'I'll fix some food for you and then see to the SOS. Don't worry about the patients. I'll look after them.'

'Okay.'

She stayed with Emma through the night, and by morning was thankful that her condition didn't seem to have worsened too much. She was sleeping a lot, and complaining still of a bad headache, but at least the vomiting had stopped. As ill as she was, she'd even managed to let Rebecca know how concerned she was to find out how her patients were getting on.

'I'm going to look in on them now,' Rebecca told her. 'I'll be back in a few minutes.'

When she went into the main room she saw that Cade was sitting with the three-year-old, wrapping a blood pressure cuff around her teddy bear's arm. The child watched him, utterly absorbed in what he was doing.

'Well, I think Teddy might be feeling a bit better this morning,' he said. 'I'm wondering if he might even like to try a cookie?'

The infant nodded cautiously. 'I'll give it to him…can I?'

'Yes, all right…if you want to… But you might have to show him how to nibble at it. What do you think?'

'Yep. I can do that.'

'Okay, then.' He handed her a plate with several cookies. 'Maybe he can eat the whole lot?'

She screwed up her nose. 'Nah.'

'Oh. Well, perhaps you'll have to help him, then?'

She nodded, picking up a biscuit and putting it to her teddy's mouth. Then she took a small bite for herself, tasting the honey and oats and deciding she liked them. Cade smiled, and Rebecca felt a lump form in her throat. He was so good with the little girl, just as he had been with the boy the day before. He would make a wonderful father.

Satisfied that the child was eating, Cade stood

up and came over to Rebecca, leaving the infant with her mother to watch over her.

'She hasn't been wanting to eat up to now,' he said, 'but I think from the looks of things she might be feeling a bit better today.'

'That's good news. You were brilliant with her, from what I could see.'

She looked around the room. The two boys were in bed, eating protein bars and doing what looked like simple crossword puzzles set out on sheets of paper.

'I thought they would keep them amused,' Cade said. 'I used to make up crosswords for William when he was little. The five-year-old can read, so he can manage simple words, and the seven-year-old is doing well with slightly harder ones. They were getting bored, but they're not strong enough to be up and about yet. Doing that and colouring pictures seemed like the best option for now.'

'You're full of surprises,' she murmured, helping herself to a few nuts and a protein bar from the selection of food he'd laid out on a table. He was a natural with the children, and they clearly liked him.

'How's Emma doing?' Cade asked.

Her mouth flattened. 'Much the same, I think. I'm worried that there's still a lot of inflammation around her brain. She's a bit confused, which would suggest things haven't improved, but at least the antibiotic seems to be keeping sepsis at bay.'

'That's something to be thankful for.' He poured some water into a glass and sipped slowly. 'We need to get everyone ready for evacuation. If the rescue helicopter arrives we should have things all packed up and set to go.'

'Yes, I've been thinking about that. I've made a start with the medication. Each adult patient should take his own treatment chart, drugs and any equipment like IV lines with him. If there's any problem—like limited numbers of passengers—then the most seriously ill should go first. My sister, the man with pneumonia, and the little girl.'

He nodded. 'With any luck the rescue team

will be here some time this morning. I've marked out a landing pad for them, where I thought it would be safest. We'll have to stretcher people over there.'

There was still no phone signal, so they had no means of knowing what to expect, but a couple of hours later they heard the heartening drone of an aircraft overhead.

The helicopter landed shortly after that. Relieved, they hurried to greet the crew.

'How many people do we have?' Cade's friend asked.

'Three children,' Cade said, 'and three adults— all of them sick—and four parents. That's ten people, plus Rebecca. She needs to go with her sister to make sure she's okay on the journey. Can you carry that many?'

'Three little ones and eight adults? Yes, we should be able to manage that.' The man frowned. 'What about yourself?'

'I need to go back down the road to get my car. I'll join you at the hospital later.' He turned to

Rebecca. 'I'll send someone to pick up the other car and take it back to the house.'

'Okay. Thanks.' She was anxious to get Emma on to the helicopter, but at the same time worried about Cade making the journey back alone. 'What if there have been more landslides? What will you do?'

He shrugged. 'I'll deal with that as it comes. You can load my medical kit on to the helicopter—you might need it, and it'll make the going quicker for me.' He made a crooked smile. 'If I don't turn up at the hospital in, say, a couple of hours, you can send William to find me with a search team.'

'I'll do that,' she said. 'You're making a joke of it, but I mean it. I didn't like the look of those rock falls on the way here.'

'Go,' he said firmly. 'Don't waste time… You need to get out of here.'

Together they supervised the transfer of all the patients on to the helicopter. Rebecca made sure Emma was secure for the flight, and then sat by her for their journey to the hospital. She was worried about her. Her sister was becoming very sleepy, and showing signs of delirium, and soon after that she deteriorated badly and started to have a seizure.

Alarmed, Rebecca quickly searched in Cade's pack for medication to control the fitting. Any seizures might increase the pressure on Emma's brain and cause her to become even more desperately ill. She had to do everything she could to stabilise her condition fast.

The pilot radioed ahead, so that when they landed on the helipad at the hospital medical teams were waiting to take care of the patients. Emma was whisked away to a treatment room where doctors took over the responsibility for her, doing everything they could to save her life. Rebecca had to stand by helplessly, watching and waiting.

Cade's friend James was the consultant in charge of her care, and he came to see Rebecca around an hour later. 'We've given her drugs to try to stop the swelling on her brain and prevent any more seizures,' he told her. 'It'll be some time before we know if the treatment's going to work. We've done tests, and now it's up to the lab to tell us if there's any other antibiotic we can use that will combat the infection more effectively.'

'Thanks, James. I know you're doing everything you possibly can.'

He nodded. 'Why don't you go to Cade's office and get a coffee? There's nothing you can do hanging around here. I'll tell Cade to come and find you when he arrives.'

'Okay.'

She went to Cade's office and phoned William to keep him up to date with what was happening before switching on the coffee machine. He was immediately concerned, both for Emma and for his cousin. 'Is he not back yet?'

'Not yet, no.'

The hot brew was reviving. She sat down on the couch and finished her drink, and then leaned her head back against the cushioned upholstery. Last night she'd watched over Emma and had hardly any sleep. She was so tired…

There was a knock on the door and then William walked into the room. 'Rebecca?' He came over to her. 'I had to come as soon as I heard. You must be worried sick.'

'Yes. There's been no more news. It could be several days before we know if she's going to be all right.'

He sat down beside her and wrapped his arms around her. 'I'm so sorry,' he said. 'I went to see her and she looks so pale...so still. I can't believe this has happened to her.'

'I know. It's a shock. But they're doing all they can.' She glanced at him. 'This must be a difficult time for you—I know you like her—and you must be so worried about your father, too. He's at this hospital, isn't he?'

'Yes, I've just come from seeing him. At least he's responding to the new medication, so we're very relieved about that.'

'I'm really pleased for you.'

He nodded. 'Emma will pull through, Becky. She's young and strong—so full of life. You and Cade were there for her, and she has every chance. She *has* to get better.'

'I hope so. I hope she's strong enough to fight it…'

Tears trickled down her cheeks and William drew her close, comforting her. She laid her head wearily against his shoulder.

Cade found them like that a few minutes later. He walked into the room and ran his glance over them in a shocked, steely, hard look that told Rebecca he'd completely misconstrued the situation.

'William.' He looked at his cousin, clearly trying to keep himself under control. 'You obviously came here as soon as you heard?'

'Yes.' William nodded. 'Becky rang me and told me what was happening. I was worried sick.'

'Of course. You two are becoming very close to one another, aren't you? You were bound to be anxious.'

Rebecca frowned, gently disentangling herself from William, and sat up, her spine rigid. 'He was worried about you, too—but you've made it back all right. I'm so glad that you're safe.'

'I'm okay. Actually, I rushed over here because I didn't want you to be on your own at a time like this…but I see I needn't have worried.' His eyes darkened as he surveyed them once more, but he kept his thoughts to himself, going over to the coffee machine.

'Becky's upset about Emma being so ill,' William said. 'I wanted to come and give her some support. I've been to see Emma…she looks very sick.'

Cade nodded. 'James tells me there's no change in her condition. We just have to wait it out.' He glanced at Rebecca. 'It's probably good news that there's been no change. It means she's stable for now.'

'Yes.' Rebecca watched him, taking in the tense lines of his body. He obviously didn't like the fact that William had been holding her—perhaps he thought that she and his cousin might get together at some point, become more serious in their relationship? He clearly didn't believe they were just friends, but this surely wasn't the time to get into a discussion about it? She was too upset about the events of the last few hours.

Emma was her priority right now—she would talk to Cade privately later. She just hoped he would listen to her.

CHAPTER SEVEN

'EMMA LOOKS A little better today, don't you think?' Rebecca glanced at Cade for confirmation and he nodded.

They'd just left the isolation room where her sister was being treated and were heading for the car park. A week had passed since Emma had been admitted to hospital, and for most of that time she had been in intensive care, sedated, and hooked up to monitors that checked her vital signs. It had been a worrying, nerve-racking time.

'She does. I think the new antibiotic must be working. James will perhaps be able to lessen the sedation soon, now that the inflammation around her brain is subsiding.'

The lab had identified the specific bacteria that were causing the problem, and for the last few days James had been able to combat the infection with a more suitable medication.

'William will be pleased,' she said. 'He's been coming with me to see her whenever he has the chance—he said he was going to see his father anyway, and felt I could do with the support.'

Cade frowned, but nodded. 'My uncle's doing well now—that's been a huge relief all round. Obviously William's still worried about him— and about Emma, too—so this news will buoy him up a bit.'

'Yes, I wanted to tell him but I couldn't get through on the phone just now.' She frowned. 'Last time I saw him he said he was going to be extra-busy this next week, because you have him overseeing the building work at the plantation.'

'That's right. I want him to make sure the carpenters stick to the drawings.'

'Is it really so important for him to keep an eye on the tradesmen the whole time? William said they all seem very good at what they do.' She studied Cade thoughtfully for a moment or two. 'I can't help thinking you're giving him this work so that he doesn't have time to be with me.'

'Do you blame me? You know how I feel about you, Rebecca…and yet you and William are so close at times.' His jaw clenched. 'You were in his arms that day at the hospital—how do you think that made me feel? It was gut-wrenching.'

'I'm sorry you felt that way.' She touched his arm lightly, in a soothing, coaxing embrace. 'William's just a friend, that's all. He was trying to comfort me.'

'Oh, yes? Is that so?' His eyes were dark with disbelief. 'I don't think William sees it that way.' His mouth made a flat line. 'I've always looked out for him—heaven knows, I want him to be happy—but I can't see him with you without wanting to break things up.'

'There's nothing going on between William and me.'

He gave her a sceptical look. 'Perhaps he just hasn't made his feelings clear to you yet. It's obvious to me that he cares about you. I saw for myself the way you two hooked up on the boat over here, and you've been to the beach together, as well as meeting up at other times and talking on the phone.'

Annoyed, she flashed him a quick dismissive glance. 'This argument is getting us nowhere,' she said tightly. 'I told you. We're just friends. I like him…he makes me laugh—and he's been good to me.'

'I don't think young men and women can have platonic relationships,' he said.

'Really? Well, that's your problem. You'll just have to deal with it the best way you can.'

He grimaced, walking with her through the main doors of the hospital. 'All right. I'll accept that you perhaps can't see what's going on with William… But I know I'm right. He has feelings for you…and I think you are more than fond of him.'

She sucked in a harsh, annoyed breath and he shot her a quick look as they crossed the car park.

'Look, perhaps we should call a truce?' he suggested. 'You've been under a huge strain this past few weeks, with everything that's happened and now your sister being ill. It would be good for you to be able to relax a bit and get some of that Caribbean holiday you came out here to enjoy. Perhaps you'd like to take some time out to have lunch with me?'

She thought about it. 'I'd like that,' she said. 'And a truce sounds good.'

He took her to a delightful restaurant a few miles along the coast. It was built on clean lines—a white stone building with wide terraces, set into the tree-covered hillside overlooking the rugged seashore.

A waiter showed them to a table in the loggia, which was decorated with tubs of glorious flame-coloured hibiscus. Rebecca sat down and looked around, immediately absorbed by the breathtaking view of the glittering blue sea. There were yachts in the harbour below, bobbing gently on the water, and in the distance she could see white-painted houses with ochre-tiled roofs dotted about the hillside.

'I've spoken to the landlord about the repairs to

the cabin,' she said, when the waiter had brought their first course to the table. She dipped her fork into a golden pastry basket and speared a tasty scallop, drizzled with a delicious Chardonnay bisque sauce. 'He says he can't get anyone out to fix the roof yet because all the tradesmen are in demand after the storm. It'll be a few more days at least—I hope you don't mind me staying at the plantation for this length of time?'

He raised dark brows. 'Of course I don't mind. You can stay as long as you like.' He smiled. 'I like having you around.'

She relaxed back in her seat, relieved. 'That's good. I don't want you to feel that I'm taking things for granted.'

'I think you worry too much,' he said. 'You were supposed to be here for a holiday, and so far you've had precious little chance to enjoy it. If I can make life easier for you in any way I will. I could take you out and about, if you want, show you the island?'

'That would be lovely,' she murmured. 'I just

need to be sure that Emma's well and truly on the mend. Maybe then I could go out with you?'

'I'll keep you to that,' he said, his mouth curving.

They finished off their starters and the main course arrived—braised lamb with risotto and roast vegetables served with a Merlot and shallot gravy.

'The food here is wonderful,' Rebecca said. 'Have you been to this restaurant before?'

He nodded. 'A few times. I've entertained suppliers here, and people who've helped me get the plantation on its feet or helped me with work on the house.'

She was relieved he hadn't mentioned bringing any other woman here. Just thinking about it made her stomach tighten.

They talked about the food, and then about the plantation and his workers. Agwe was on the mend, he said. 'He's been fortunate—the illness hasn't done any permanent damage to his kidneys. And Thomas's hand is healing up nicely.'

'I'm pleased for both of them. They're lucky

to have an employer who looks after them and takes their welfare so seriously.'

They finished off their meal with a fruit dessert, followed by cups of richly flavoured Columbian coffee accompanied by thin dark chocolate wafers.

'I'm so full,' Rebecca said, rubbing her stomach. 'I haven't eaten such a great meal for ages. That was perfect.'

He paid the bill and they left the restaurant, walking at his suggestion through the botanical gardens that covered the hillside. They passed along a trail where avocados and apricot trees grew in abundance, alongside hanging bird-of-paradise flowers and flamboyant heliconia that attracted the attention of tiny hummingbirds searching for nectar.

It was incredibly peaceful out here, and in the tropical heat of the late afternoon they stood for a while on a small wooden bridge over a large lily pond and watched the parrots flit among the trees. Cade put his arm around her and pointed to where bright pink flamingos paraded at the side of the pool. One female was feeding its youngster—a small bird that was pure white.

'Oh, aren't they beautiful?' she exclaimed softly. 'The chicks are adorable.'

He laughed softly. 'So are you,' he said, hugging her close and dropping a kiss on her startled lips. 'It's great to see you looking happy.'

She looked up at him in wonder, still dazed by the unexpected gentleness of that kiss. Her lips tingled with excitement and her heart leapt, her pulses racing in anticipation that he might do it again. Slowly, bending his head towards her, he obliged, brushing her mouth with his, sending a trail of fire to course through every part of her body.

She wanted more—wanted to have him holding her and running his hands over her, tugging her to him. And even as the thoughts entered her head, he satisfied her inner yearning, tenderly shaping her body with his palms.

She kissed him hungrily, lifting her arms and running her fingers over the corded muscles of his shoulders. 'You've been so good to me…'

she whispered. 'Taking care of me, offering me a place to stay…I've never met anyone who's been so generous, so thoughtful.'

'I think the world of you,' he said. 'In fact…I think I've fallen in love with you. I've never felt this way before, nor met anyone quite like you, and ever since I first met you I've never stopped wanting you.' His voice was husky, ragged. 'If you knew how you make me feel you would take me into your heart and trust me. I would never hurt you—you need to know that.'

It was what she wanted to hear more than anything. She lifted a hand to his face, stroking his cheek, running her fingers lightly along his hard jawline. 'I wish I could be sure of that,' she said quietly. 'I wish I knew how to make things turn out the way I want. I can't. But I do wish things were different.'

He frowned, and she suddenly realised he might have misinterpreted her words.

'You mean you're still not sure about whether you want to keep your options open? If you're only with me because you're grateful for the way I've looked after you—'

'No, it isn't like that—' she interrupted, but she didn't have the chance to talk to him about it any more because suddenly, alerted by footsteps in the distance and chattering voices, they realised that they were no longer alone.

They moved apart as other visitors to the gardens approached, coming out from the arbour and moving towards the pond.

Wordlessly Rebecca and Cade walked to the other side of the bridge and followed a path through the lush undergrowth on the route back to the car park.

When they were alone once again he drew in a deep breath and said, 'I can't help the way I feel about you, Rebecca. I was lost the moment I first saw you.'

'But—'

He put a finger to her lips, stopping the flow of words. 'There's a barbecue on the beach in a few days' time. I thought you might like to go with me?'

'Yes, that sounds good.' She smiled at him tentatively.

There was little point in arguing with him, in pointing out where his thinking was flawed. And she *wanted* to be with him. Her efforts to keep him at bay all this time had been for nothing, because she had well and truly fallen for him. She had to admit it to herself. He was everything she wanted in a man, but she wasn't sure how it had happened that she'd come to love him.

How could it ever be right for her to be with him—knowing that she might never be able to give him the family he wanted? She wasn't being fair to him, letting this go on, and yet she couldn't bear *not* to be with him.

She had to find a way to sort things out, to come to terms with the kind of future she might have. Was it possible for her ever to be with Cade?

Over the next few days Emma gradually gained strength and was able to sit up in bed. Before too long she was even able to chat without getting too tired.

'You're looking so much better,' Rebecca told her. 'I'm so glad you're on the mend.'

'It's you I have to thank for that,' Emma said, leaning back against her pillows.

'Hmm…I think there's more to it than that,' Rebecca murmured.

She looked at the bedside table, bright with colourful flowers and cards from well-wishers. There was one, she noticed, from William—an especially beautiful embossed card, inscribed with affectionate sentiment.

She looked closely at Emma. Her sister's long chestnut hair had regained some of its sheen and her blue-grey eyes were bright. 'Could that sparkle in your eyes be due to the fact that you've had a handsome young man visiting you every day while you've been here?'

Emma blushed. 'You noticed? It's true—William's been coming to see me every chance he gets. He brings me fruit and flowers, and he's doing everything he can to cheer me up.' She glanced at the bedside locker. 'He brought me those beautiful roses, and there's a note with them that says he's thinking of me always.'

'Well, well…isn't *that* a lovely turn of events? How do you feel about him?'

Emma's cheeks reddened even further. 'I really like him, Becky. He has such a good sense of humour, and we have so much in common. I think we clicked the first time we met.' She studied Rebecca thoughtfully. 'You feel the same way about his cousin, don't you? I've seen the signs, and I'm pretty sure you're in love with Cade?'

'What makes you think that?'

'I saw the way you looked at him when he came to the cabin—*and* when we were at Selwyn's Bar. You were laughing and joking with William, but it was Cade you were watching when you thought no one was looking. And I've seen it when you've both been here to visit me.' Her mouth made a crooked shape. 'To be honest, I don't think men can see beyond their noses.'

Rebecca sighed. That was true enough. Cade

wouldn't listen when she told him she and William were just good friends.

'I don't know what to do, Emma. Yes, it's true—I do love Cade. And I know he feels the same way about me. But there's no future for us, is there? How can I be with him if I can't have children? He says he wants a family, and I can't deny him that. I don't know what to do.'

'There's one thing you can do.' Emma reached for her sister's hand. 'Go for treatment...have surgery to try to open your fallopian tubes.'

Rebecca frowned. 'But the doctors back home weren't keen on that—they said it's not done very often. They told me my best prospect would be to try in vitro fertilisation in the future—and that will depend on my ovaries being unaffected by the scar tissue...which they aren't. Besides, IVF isn't always successful. You hear of people having several courses without a good result.'

'That's a negative way of thinking. You're better than that, Becky. You were always a positive person until this happened to you. If you're worried about IVF you should go and make an appointment at a clinic—talk to someone about having specialised surgery to open up your fallopian tubes and remove any scar tissue that's causing a problem. What's the point of waiting? Not knowing if there is anything you can do about it is making you put your life on hold.'

'I suppose you're right.' Rebecca tried to think things through. 'I'll think about it. It's such a big step, though.' She closed her eyes briefly. 'I think I've been putting it off in case it doesn't work.'

'Don't just think about it. Do it. At least then you'll know definitely, won't you? And then you'll be in a position to make proper decisions about your future. At the moment you're in limbo.' Emma squeezed her hand. 'Don't waste any more time, Becky. In fact—pass me my handbag from the bedside locker, will you? I did some research when I knew you were coming over to stay for a while. There's a clinic on one of the islands that would be just right for you. I checked into them and they're really good, by all accounts. The surgeons there are really skilled.'

Rebecca did as she asked and Emma fetched a card out of her bag.

'Here. Give them a ring,' she said. 'Do it today. They told me they should be able to fit you in at short notice if you're a private patient.' She frowned. 'And for goodness' sake talk to Cade.'

Rebecca shook her head. 'I can't do it now—not while you're still in hospital. What if they can do it straight away? I would be so worried about you. I'll ring them in a few weeks...when you're up and about.'

'No, no... There's no time like the present. I want you to do it now...I'm feeling so much better. I'm not in danger any more, and with any luck by the time I'm out of here you'll be back from the clinic, so we can spend some time together at the cabin. You might only need an overnight stay in hospital. Rebecca—call them and make an appointment.' She smiled. 'William will be here to keep me company when he's not at the plantation. You don't need to worry about me.'

'I can't. Not now. I need to be here with *you*.'

'Those are just excuses.' Emma pursed her lips determinedly. 'I'll do it for you.' She started to reach for her phone.

'No, don't do that.'

Rebecca looked at the card once more. The clinic was situated on an island nearby—just a ferry ride away. She *could* do it, couldn't she? At least then she would know if things were ever going to be all right for her, wouldn't she?

'Okay,' she sighed. 'I'll do it. I'll give them a call.'

'Good. Put it on speaker phone so I can hear what they say.'

Rebecca dialled the number on the card.

'You're in luck,' the receptionist at the clinic said, when Rebecca had introduced herself and explained the situation. 'We've had a couple of cancellations—one patient has a family crisis to deal with and another has decided to try an alternative treatment—so Mr Solomon has some free time. I can book you in to see him tomorrow, if you like? That will be an initial appointment, and he'll arrange any other details with you when you see him.'

Rebecca shook her head. That was far too soon. 'I wasn't expecting to be seen so quickly,' she said. 'I'm not sure—'

'She'll do it,' Emma said, cutting in on the conversation. 'Make the appointment, please.'

'Madam?'

'Sorry, that's my sister…adding her two pennyworth.' Rebecca took a deep breath. 'Okay, then. Thank you. I'll come in tomorrow. We'll take it from there.'

She cut the call a couple of minutes later and sat quietly for a bit longer, getting over the enormity of what she was doing. She had to think of practicalities. There would be a ferry later today. If she hurried she could throw a few things into her holdall and be on her way. Once she arrived on the island she could think about booking a hotel room near to the clinic.

'I came over to the Caribbean to see you and to ask your advice,' she said, looking at Emma. 'I knew you'd know what I should do.' She gave

Emma a hug. 'You're my best big sister,' she said. 'I love you to bits.' Glancing at her once again, she added, 'And now look what I've done—I've tired you out with all this talking. I'm sorry.'

'I'll be fine.' Emma smiled. 'I'm feeling so much better now…and I'm getting up and walking about a bit every day… But they say they want to keep me in for several more days to be certain everything's all right.' She sent her a meaningful look. 'Time enough for you to have the surgery,' she said. 'You can call me from the clinic.'

They talked for a minute or two longer and then Rebecca stood up to leave. 'I'll go and see if I can find Cade,' she said.

She found him in the main area of the Emergency Unit, talking with a man and woman who were standing by the main desk. He had his back to her, but she went up to him and laid a hand lightly on his arm.

'Hi, I've just been up to Emma's room and I thought I'd come down here to see you, if you're not too busy.'

'I'm never to busy to see you,' he said, turning to face her.

He was smiling, obviously in a good mood, and she suddenly recognised the couple with him.

'It's Mr and Mrs Tennyson, isn't it?' she said, her eyes widening.

'That's right. We wanted to come in and thank everyone for looking after us so well…and especially to thank Dr Byfield for saving Annie.'

They both looked well—much better than when she'd seen them last, when Jane Tennyson had been suffering with broken ribs after the car accident and her husband Paul had been concussed from his head injury.

'You seem to be recovering well,' Cade said.

'Oh, yes, we're on the mend,' Jane said happily. 'My ribs are healing, and Paul is just fine. And as for little Annie—she's doing brilliantly.'

'I'm so pleased she's recovered.' Rebecca looked around. 'Where is she? Is she not with you today?'

'Oh, she's here.' Jane smiled broadly. 'The

nurses were so happy to see her they whisked her away to show her off to everyone. Here she is now.'

Greta was carrying Annie back to them. The little girl looked the picture of health, and she put her arms out to Cade to be picked up. She moved her fingers impatiently, wanting his attention.

Paul Tennyson chuckled. 'Oh, she can't get enough of you. You're her favourite person today.'

Cade smiled and took Annie into his arms, giving her a cuddle. 'You're a real cherub, aren't you?' he said. He tickled the little girl's tummy and she giggled.

Watching them, Rebecca felt her heart contract with pain. She longed to hold the infant herself, but didn't trust herself not to break down. She wouldn't want to give her back.

'She's gorgeous,' she said, trying to keep a firm lid on her emotions.

Cade was jiggling the little girl gently up and

down and she was laughing, loving the sensation and wanting more.

'Again!' Annie squealed with delight. 'Again.'

'Enough, sweetheart,' Cade said after a minute or two. 'Your mum wants to hold you.' He handed her to her mother and the trio said their goodbyes and went on their way.

He turned to Rebecca. 'We'll go into my office. We're having a quiet time in Emergency just now.' As he led the way he said, 'It was great seeing them now that they're more or less back to normal, wasn't it?'

She nodded, trying to get a grip on herself. He sent her an odd look. 'What is it, Rebecca?' He opened the door to his office and ushered her inside. 'Has something happened? Is there something you want to talk to me about?'

'I… Yes…' She took a deep breath.

She'd wanted to talk to him about them maybe having a future together, but seeing him with the infant had thrown her into a quandary. What if her treatment was unsuccessful? How could she put him though that?

'I've decided to go away for a few days,' she said finally. 'I'm going over to Barbados for a short break.'

His dark brows drew together. 'When are you going? I could perhaps get some time off and go with you.'

'No…I'm going today. I've made up my mind… It was a spur-of-the-moment decision and I'm getting the ferry later this afternoon.'

'I don't understand.' He looked bewildered. 'Why would you leave when your sister's still in the hospital?'

'She's…she's feeling much better now… She thinks I don't need to worry about her…and she'll have William to keep her company.'

His frown deepened. 'Wait a minute… That's what this is about, isn't it? It's about William. Is he with Emma? I had hoped you were over him—that you might—'

'I've *never* had any romantic feelings for William,' she said, cutting Cade off unexpectedly. 'I told you, I like him as a friend. It's you I want… I love *you*…'

He drew in a sharp breath and she went on hurriedly.

'I didn't mean for it to happen, and I tried to stop it, but it just… It's impossible—I can't love you, Cade. It would be wrong for us. It wouldn't work out.'

'But *why* wouldn't it?' He was bewildered. 'We're so good together, Rebecca. And now that you've told me that you love me, too, what's to stop us?' He drew her to him, kissing her fiercely, as though he couldn't bear to let her go. 'We'd be perfect together.' He murmured the words against her mouth. 'I love you.'

The kiss was her undoing. Her lips softened under the tender onslaught and her whole body quivered as he ran his hands over her, shaping her to him. 'I know your ex let you down,' he said in a roughened voice, 'but don't let him come between us. I love you…you say you love me…what could possibly be wrong?'

An alarm bell started to ring in the Emergency Unit and a nurse's voice came over the speaker system to say that a patient was being brought in by ambulance. Cade stiffened, but didn't let her go.

Rebecca laid a shaky hand on his chest. 'Cade, the truth is you've told me you want a family and I don't think I can give you that. I told you I was ill, and there's a lot of scar tissue…adhesions. My doctors have said they don't think I'll be able to conceive. I don't want to put you through that. It wouldn't be fair to deny you something you've always dreamed of.'

He was staring down at her, a shocked look on his face. 'You can't have children? That's a *terrible* diagnosis. Why on earth didn't you tell me this before?'

Before he'd fallen in love with her?

'I don't know—I'm not sure. It was painful for me and I couldn't face up to it. The time never seemed right. I was too busy trying to stop myself from falling for you.'

'Was that because of how your ex reacted?'

She nodded. 'After I told Drew what the doctors had said he went away for a while to think things through. Then he told me he'd thought long and hard about it but he couldn't stay with me if there was the possibility of my not having children.' Her face crumpled. 'I couldn't bear to have you say that to me. I'm sorry.'

A muscle flicked in his jaw. 'We need to talk about this,' he said. 'It's such a shock…coming out of the blue like this. I'd no idea.' He frowned. 'Look, I have to go and deal with this emergency, but we have to talk some more.' He stared at her, his eyes smoke-dark, flickering with a troubled mixture of pain and anger. 'You should have told me, Rebecca.'

'I know. I'm sorry.'

He left her, reluctantly, to go and deal with the patient who was being brought in, and Rebecca made her way out of the hospital, went back to the plantation.

Once there, she quickly packed a bag and called for a taxi. She wasn't going to use Cade's car any more. It wouldn't be right. She would have to send for the rest of her things at a later date.

Things were surely over between them. He'd

been utterly shocked and dismayed by her revelation, and all the talking in the world wouldn't make things come right. He deserved better. He deserved to find happiness with a woman who could give him the family he wanted. This was her burden to bear. It didn't have to be his.

She hurried out of the house as the taxi driver pulled up outside. 'Where to, miss?' he asked.

'The ferry port,' she said.

She looked back at the house as they drove away and inside she felt as though her heart was breaking.

CHAPTER EIGHT

REBECCA OPENED HER eyes and looked around the unfamiliar room. For a moment or two she was disorientated and couldn't remember where she was, but then a nurse approached the bedside and smiled.

'Oh, you're back with us! You came round from surgery and then went to sleep for a couple of hours. How are you feeling?'

'I'm okay...I think.'

'Good. It'll take some time for the effects of the anaesthetic to wear off, but you don't need to do anything. Just rest for a while. I'll take your blood pressure.' The nurse wrapped the cuff around Rebecca's upper arm and checked the monitor. 'It's a little low,' she said after a moment or two, 'but that's to be expected after surgery.'

'Do you know anything about how the surgery went?' Still a little groggy, Rebecca struggled to sit up in bed. She was a bit sore from the procedure she'd undergone, and there was a dressing on her tummy where the surgeon had stitched up a small incision.

'Dr Solomon will be in to explain things to you in a little while,' the nurse said. 'You were so fortunate to have him as your surgeon—he's a brilliant man—very skilled at doing tubal surgery.'

'So I've been told.' Perhaps it was the after-effects of the general anaesthetic, but Rebecca was feeling overwhelmed, and above all isolated and lonely. She was on her own in this—but then she'd known that from the beginning, hadn't she?

She tried to put a brave face on things, but the nurse must have guessed how she was feeling, because she said, 'How about a cup of tea? That should help to cheer you up.'

'Thanks. That would be lovely.'

'Oh, and you have a visitor… Are you up to seeing anyone yet?'

'A visitor?' Rebecca echoed.

Who could that be? No one knew she was here except for Emma. She'd phoned her sister yesterday, to tell her that the surgery was being done on a day-patient basis—the doctor had found an operating theatre slot for the day after her first appointment. He'd said that if all was well she would be able to leave hospital about four hours after the procedure.

'Oh, yes. He said he came over on the ferry this morning. Looks like a dark thundercloud, but gorgeous with it. He's been here since you went to theatre, pacing up and down, wearing a hole in the waiting room floor. Mind you…' The nurse grinned. 'He could come and pace *my* floor any time!'

'Cade's here? Dr Byfield?'

'That's the one. That'll be two cups of tea, then, will it?'

Rebecca nodded, still trying to take it in. What

was he doing here? How had he known where to find her?

The nurse left the room and a moment later Cade came through the door. He stood by the doorjamb, studying her, not saying a word, his face taut, his expression one of controlled anger.

She swallowed apprehensively. 'I wasn't expecting to see you,' she said in a quiet voice. 'Come in and sit by the bed. How did you know where to find me?'

He strode towards the bed, but ignored her offer of a seat. 'I asked Emma where you'd be. She was surprised you hadn't told me. So was I. I thought we were going to talk. Yet you took off without another word.'

'Okay. Okay, I'm sorry.' She looked at him doubtfully. 'We can talk now, if you want.'

'It's a bit late, isn't it…? A bit overdue? I can't imagine why you would leave like that, without saying anything or telling me where you were going. What were you *thinking*?'

She frowned. 'I don't know, exactly. What's the point in talking if I might not be able to have children? I may have to get used to the idea, but you don't.'

'So you walked out on me? You decided I didn't need to know what was going on—that I wouldn't want any part of it?' His jaw was clenched, his mouth a flat, harsh line. 'I told you I would help you any way I can—that I would always be there for you. Did you think they were just meaningless words?'

She gave a half-hearted shrug. 'People say all sorts of things on the spur of the moment, when nothing much is at stake. Drew promised he'd love me for ever, but that fizzled out a very short time after I became ill.'

'I'm not Drew. It's high time you stopped comparing me to him.'

'But you made it very clear to me that you want children—that you want a large family to make up for what you missed out on in the past. I couldn't be certain of giving you that—what was I supposed to think or do?'

'You should have talked it through with me. Yes, I want a family—but I've fallen in love with you, Rebecca… How can I ignore that? Do you *really* think I'm the kind of man who will reject you because you can't give me everything I want? Do you *really* think I'm that selfish?'

Her shoulders lifted. 'I don't know what to think. Are you going to sit down or not? Did you just come here to quarrel with me?' she queried grumpily. 'Because I can pick a fight with myself—I don't need you to do it for me.'

He laughed—a short, sharp sound that cracked on the air. 'No, I'm sorry.' Finally he pulled up a chair and sat down beside her. 'I came to see how you are…and to make you see that I'm nothing like your ex. I *will* be here for you, Rebecca, no matter what happens.'

She swallowed against the lump that had suddenly formed in her throat. A sheen of tears misted her eyes. 'I never expected that,' she said in a muffled voice. 'I'm so glad you're here, Cade.'

She put out a hand to him and he grasped it reassuringly, enclosing her palm in his long fingers, resting their entwined hands on the bedcovers.

'So how did the surgery go?' he asked.

'I don't know,' she admitted. 'They haven't told me yet. The surgeon will be in later to see me.'

The nurse came in with a tea tray and set it down on the bedside table. 'There you are. Help yourselves. Mr Solomon will be here soon. He's just talking to another patient.'

'Thanks.'

'You're welcome.' She glanced at the monitor. 'Your heartrate's gone up in the last few minutes.' She waggled an admonishing finger. 'Not good.' Then she glanced at Cade and sighed. 'But hardly surprising, really.' She sniffed and left the room.

Rebecca laughed, and then held on to her tummy, where the stitches were under pressure. 'She thinks you're gorgeous,' she said.

He raised a dark brow. 'Oh? And what do *you* think?'

'I think you're pretty wonderful, all told. I just don't want you to get swell-headed about it.'

'There's not much likelihood of that. I don't have time to be swayed by what people think. I'm a very practical kind of man. I like to know where I stand, make plans and see them through.'

'That can be difficult. Things don't always go to plan.'

'That's true.'

There was a knock on the door and Mr Solomon walked into the room. He was a tall man, dressed in an immaculate dark suit.

'Hello,' he said, smiling. 'It's good to see you sitting up and with a bit more colour in your cheeks. Is it all right if I come in and talk to you about the results of your surgery?'

'Yes, please. Come in. Sit down.'

Cade glanced at her. 'Would you prefer it if I leave? I can wait outside.'

She shook her head. 'No, it's all right. I'd like you to stay.'

Mr Solomon sat down. His expression became

serious and Rebecca immediately sensed trouble. She watched him, her shoulders stiff, trying to prepare herself for what was to come. It didn't look good.

'You'll recall we talked about the tests we did yesterday?' he said, and she nodded. 'There were a lot of adhesions around your ovaries and both fallopian tubes, and the hysterosalpingogram showed us that the tubes weren't viable in that state.'

'Yes...' It was almost a whisper.

'As we discussed, with that much scarring it's not always easy to remedy the situation, but we went ahead and did as much as we could.'

'And the result?'

'The good news is that one of your ovaries is now completely clear...'

She sighed with relief. It meant that IVF might be an option at least.

'Also, one of your fallopian tubes was blocked at the uterine end, which was good as far as we were concerned, because it was easier to clear.

So, it means that with one fallopian tube and a functional ovary your chances of conceiving a baby are much better than they were before you came to see us.' He frowned. 'There is a possibility, though, that the surgery in itself might cause more scarring. But at the moment I'd say you have a forty to fifty per cent chance of getting pregnant.'

She smiled. That was so much better than no chance at all. 'Thank you, Mr Solomon. I'm really grateful for everything you've done…and for seeing me so quickly.'

'I'm glad to have helped…and I had a cancellation so there was no problem getting you into theatre.' He checked the monitors. 'We'll check your blood pressure and temperature again, and when they're satisfactory, we'll let you go. The nurse will go through your aftercare instructions with you. Any problems at all—come back to us.'

'Thanks again, Doctor.'

He left the room and she sat with Cade, waiting for the news to sink in.

'It isn't perfect,' she said. 'But it's better than I expected.'

He squeezed her hand. 'I'm glad for you, Rebecca. You did the right thing, coming here. But you should have told me. You should have trusted me. You should always have faith in me.'

He kissed her gently on the mouth, and then leaned back in his chair as the nurse came back into the room.

'I need to check your blood pressure again,' she said, 'and then we'll see about sending you home.'

Rebecca left the hospital with Cade a few hours later. They took a taxi to the ferry port and managed to time things just right, with the boat leaving for St Marie-Rose shortly after that.

The crossing was smooth, the sea a tranquil, glassy blue. They sat by the deck rail, looking out at the coastline, sipping ice-cold mango juice and eating cool slices of melon.

'How do you feel?' Cade asked. 'Did they say

anything about how long it will take you to recover from the surgery?'

'I'm feeling okay. It shouldn't take too long at all, really. I'll probably be back to normal in a couple of days.'

'That's good. We'll get you settled in back at the house and you can rest up as much as you need. I'll take you to see Emma whenever I can, or I'll arrange for Benjamin to take you there and bring you back.'

'That's good. Thank you…I can't wait to see her.' She frowned. 'I should be with her when she goes home to the cabin. She'll need someone with her for a few weeks while she's convalescing.'

'Erm…and what about *you*? You've just had an operation yourself, so you'll both need some looking after! Why don't you both stay at the plantation house? There's plenty of room, and you'll be a lot more comfortable there, I expect…and Harriet will love being able to cook for more than just me.'

'I'll ask her.' She smiled at him and laid her hand on his. 'Thank you…again.'

A week later she was starting to feel a little better. The small laparoscopy wound was healing up and she had managed to visit Emma earlier in the day. She had been greeted with the news that she was soon going to be able to come home.

'Stay at the plantation house?' Emma had been thrilled by the invitation. 'Oh, wow! That sounds fantastic…and I'll be so much nearer to William, won't I? He says he has a cottage not far from there. Oh, it gets better and better. I can't wait to get out of here.'

Cade had already started to move Emma's things from the cabin to the plantation house. He seemed to like having a house full of people. He'd told Rebecca to pick out a room for her sister and that he'd do whatever she wanted to make her comfortable there.

Now, though, Rebecca was getting ready to go out for the evening with him.

'There's that barbecue on the beach, remember?' he'd said earlier. 'It starts just before sun-set and goes on till people start leaving.' He grinned. 'I think it's time for you to have some fun. If you're feeling up to it, of course?'

'Yay!'

She didn't know what to wear, but in the end picked out a colourful sarong that had a thin halter-neck strap and left her shoulders bare. It wrapped around her, nipping in at the waist and gliding over her hips in soft folds, and gave a glimpse of a long tanned thigh as she walked. She'd pinned her hair up, so that curls massed around the back of her head and fell in gentle tendrils to frame her face.

When she had finished dressing she went downstairs, ready to leave as soon as the taxi arrived at the front of the house. Cade had been looking around for his house keys, but when he saw her approach he stopped what he was doing and stared at her, transfixed.

'Oh...Rebecca... Oh...you look stunning.' His dark gaze moved over her as though he was captivated by the vision before him. 'You look so lovely…'

'I'm glad you think so.' She ran a hand over the sarong. 'I wasn't sure what people wear at these parties.'

'Whatever they wear, you'll be the most beautiful girl there. I won't dare let you out of my sight for an instant.'

She laughed and went out with him to the waiting cab. The driver whisked them away, stopping to drop them off at the shore a few minutes later.

They walked on to the sand and watched the setting sun dip slowly on the horizon, casting an arc of gold over the blue sky. Palm fronds waved gently in the light breeze and gradually the sky turned a dusky pink.

Behind them the bartender had opened up his wooden shack and was serving fruity rum punch and piña coladas. At the same time the chef had fired up the barbecue, so that soon the aroma of steak and chicken filled the air. People were soon queuing up to sample tasty titbits.

'Try these jerk chicken wraps,' Cade said, taking her over to where a buffet table had been set out. 'They're delicious.'

She tasted them, along with seafood skewers and spicy roast pork. 'Mmm…mmm…mmm…' she said. 'You're right. Everything tastes wonderful. I *love* Caribbean food. And I definitely want to try those coconut kisses for dessert.'

The musicians struck up a rhythm on their steel drums and people started to dance, swaying in time with the music. Cade led Rebecca on to a flat stretch of sand and for a while they moved together to the sound of calypso and reggae.

As the sky darkened and the moon glittered on the sea he held her close and kissed her tenderly. 'I love you,' he said. 'Will you marry me?'

'I love you, too,' she said softly, her heart leaping with joy at the unexpected proposal. 'And I want to marry you more than anything in the world.'

He pulled in a quick, shaky breath, his face lighting up in a smile. He lowered his head and kissed her passionately on the mouth. She clung to him, wrapping her arms around him.

'Have you thought this through?' she asked after a while, when they came up for air. 'I've had the surgery, but it isn't a guarantee that everything will be all right.'

'I want to be with you,' he said simply, taking her by the hand and leading her by the water's edge. 'If children come along, that will be wonderful. But if they don't…we could go for adoption or find some other way of satisfying that need.'

He looked at her.

'It's early days, but perhaps you should think about going back to working with children—even if it's only part-time? You have a lot to give, Rebecca. You've had a lot to think about these last few months—this year—but now you have a chance to be happy again. We *both* have that chance.'

'I could be happy with you,' she said. 'Being with you is what I want more than anything.'

He slid his arm around her waist and they

walked along the beach, the sound of steel drums floating on the air, the fading light dancing on the water.

'We'll be good together,' he said. 'I feel it inside. It's as though I've been waiting for you to come along my whole life.'

They stood in the shelter of a coconut palm and he took her in his arms. His kisses filled her with exhilaration and made her body tingle with joyful anticipation.

There was a lifetime of love ahead of them. She knew it.

EPILOGUE

'REBECCA, THE CATERER wants to know where to put the large fruit basket.'

Cade was frowning and Rebecca smiled. For a man who was so good at dealing with emergencies and handling people, he was being strangely inept when it came to dealing with the intricacies of organising his cousin's wedding.

Of course he'd had more than usual to contend with these last few days, with the plantation house full of guests. Her family had come over to the Caribbean to stay for a few weeks, and his family was here, too.

'Tell her I thought it would look good on the end table,' she said. 'The one at the far end of the marquee.'

'Okay.' He came over to her and placed a hand lightly on her tummy. 'How's the bump doing today? Oh…he's kicking.' His mouth curved and he stayed very still for a while, waiting for his son to move around some more.

'Yes, he is.' She laid her left hand on top of his, the gold wedding band glinting brightly in the sunlight that streamed in through the windows. 'He's been doing that all morning. It must be all the excitement, and I think he's feeling cramped in there…only four more weeks to go.' She sighed, looking down at her large abdomen. 'Trust William and Emma to decide to get married when I'm as big as this—I wanted to wear something special for their big day.'

He placed a gentle kiss on her soft lips. 'You look lovely. And think of it this way—at least our boy will be at his auntie's wedding.'

She laughed. 'Okay, I'll grant you that. But let's hope we get the timing right with the next one.'

He wrapped his arms around her and kissed her tenderly. 'Of course we will. It'll be perfect, I promise you. When our children come along the timing will always be right.'

* * * * *

MILLS & BOON®
Large Print Medical

September

The Socialite's Secret	Carol Marinelli
London's Most Eligible Doctor	Annie O'Neil
Saving Maddie's Baby	Marion Lennox
A Sheikh to Capture Her Heart	Meredith Webber
Breaking All Their Rules	Sue MacKay
One Life-Changing Night	Louisa Heaton

October

Seduced by the Heart Surgeon	Carol Marinelli
Falling for the Single Dad	Emily Forbes
The Fling That Changed Everything	Alison Roberts
A Child to Open Their Hearts	Marion Lennox
The Greek Doctor's Secret Son	Jennifer Taylor
Caught in a Storm of Passion	Lucy Ryder

November

Tempted by Hollywood's Top Doc	Louisa George
Perfect Rivals...	Amy Ruttan
English Rose in the Outback	Lucy Clark
A Family for Chloe	Lucy Clark
The Doctor's Baby Secret	Scarlet Wilson
Married for the Boss's Baby	Susan Carlisle

MILLS & BOON®
Large Print Medical

December

The Prince and the Midwife	Robin Gianna
His Pregnant Sleeping Beauty	Lynne Marshall
One Night, Twin Consequences	Annie O'Neil
Twin Surprise for the Single Doc	Susanne Hampton
The Doctor's Forbidden Fling	Karin Baine
The Army Doc's Secret Wife	Charlotte Hawkes

January

Taming Hollywood's Ultimate Playboy	Amalie Berlin
Winning Back His Doctor Bride	Tina Beckett
White Wedding for a Southern Belle	Susan Carlisle
Wedding Date with the Army Doc	Lynne Marshall
Capturing the Single Dad's Heart	Kate Hardy
Doctor, Mummy...Wife?	Dianne Drake

February

Seduced by the Sheikh Surgeon	Carol Marinelli
Challenging the Doctor Sheikh	Amalie Berlin
The Doctor She Always Dreamed Of	Wendy S. Marcus
The Nurse's Newborn Gift	Wendy S. Marcus
Tempting Nashville's Celebrity Doc	Amy Ruttan
Dr White's Baby Wish	Sue MacKay